to the bridge

To the Bridge

a novel

Yasuko Thanh

HAMISH HAMILTON

an imprint of Penguin Canada, a division of Penguin Random House Canada Limited

Canada • USA • UK • Ireland • Australia • New Zealand • India • South Africa • China

First published 2023

www.penguinrandomhouse.ca

*Publisher's note: This book is a work of fiction. Names, characters, places and incidents
either are the product of the author's imagination or are used fictitiously, and any
resemblance to actual persons living or dead, events, or locales is entirely coincidental.*

*The author wishes to acknowledge the support of the Canada Council
for the Arts and the BC Arts Council.*

LIBRARY AND ARCHIVES CANADA CATALOGUING IN PUBLICATION

Title: To the bridge : a novel / Yasuko Thanh.
Names: Thanh, Yasuko, author.
Identifiers: Canadiana (print) 20220423431 | Canadiana (ebook) 20220423458 |
ISBN 9780735244672 (softcover) | ISBN 9780735244689 (EPUB)
Classification: LCC PS8639.H375 T6 2023 | DDC C813/.6—dc23

Book design by Kate Sinclair
Cover design by Kate Sinclair
Cover images: (cut paper) © MirageC / Getty Images; (waves) *Crashing Waves*,
oil on canvas, Alfred Thompson Bricher (1837-1908)

Printed in Canada

10 9 8 7 6 5 4 3 2 1

Penguin
Random House
HAMISH HAMILTON CANADA

for Talitha

But behind all your stories is always your mother's story,
because hers is where yours begins.

—Mitch Albom, *For One More Day*

one

When my mother died, I used to wonder how anyone could become so broken that they'd want to end their own life. Now I'm a mother myself, at this mathematical point in time, waking in alarm, the digital clock screaming "*Wah-wah-wah*. Get up, get up, your life is shit: you're not making enough money, not making enough love, not making good. You're late for something. *Wah-wah-wah*."

Then I'm in a hospital bathroom with handrails, Juliet on the toilet, pee tinkling in the bowl. "You've heard of a thing called privacy, right?"

"You surrendered your right to privacy when you tried to kill yourself." I say those words, "kill yourself," aloud for the first time.

"There's nothing for me to kill myself *with* in here," Juliet says, wiping in disgust, flushing, pushing her IV pole back to bed. "You're making too big a deal of this."

She tangles herself in the tubing, cannula bruises on her arm like the defence wounds of an assault victim, and as I help her manoeuvre onto the mattress I say, "Stealing a tube of lipstick is not a big deal. Failing an exam. Staying out all night. But life and death? That's as big a deal as it gets."

"What-ev." A sadness, the sadness of having survived, passes over her face. Then she's back to smiling as though this is a gory horror movie she's watching, not starring in.

I will remember the two of us, my daughter and I, sitting on her bedroom carpet at home. Her face green-seeming in the morning light. Haloed like an apocryphal angel. I will, in years to come, recall her lips not moving but her voice clear as a bird. "Last chance to dance. Bet it all. Let it ride." I will recall Juliet's birth, her hand in mine. I will learn that a day can start out as utterly ordinary and then transform itself in such a manner that by dusk you realize everything you love can be taken away.

A day before the grind began, I turned off the alarm clock and lay in bed asking myself unrhetorically how it would feel to wake up happy for a change. Because as much as growing older meant admitting certain of my dreams had best-before dates, I'd dusted off my long-range lenses and begun to circle the globe with my finger for the first time in years.

My husband Syd wrangled the recycling in his bathrobe. I turned the coffee on, and fought the urge to smoke a cigarette on the front step, making myself believe I didn't want one, though the first cigarette of the day was always the best one, and the hardest to give up—mist all around, a breeze rattling the wind chime, seagulls squawking—then wrestled the garbage bin down the rutted driveway, a good mother anchored, in the words of Sophocles, to life. 3

I was determined to see Juliet succeed. She was everything good in the world. Great, even. And to see something I'd brought into the world be great justified my investment as a parent. Juliet was on a scholarship track to university. "Apply everywhere," I'd encouraged. "Give yourself the broadest range of choices." Our family had had its troubles, but in ten months she'd be gone and her old bedroom would become my darkroom, or a storage room for the mid-century clothes I sold online, anything. Syd and I had made it through the tunnel; we could see the light of freedom. Freedom. Well, I'd just throw myself at life and see what I stuck to, what stuck to me, the thing I wanted most also being what scared me the most.

I shuffled back inside past a pile of flip-flops, hoodies on hooks, snagging my foot on the brown and yellow shag rug, catching myself on the wooden cradle holding gumboots.

Juliet opened her door a crack. "Can I talk to you a minute?" Her body faded into the perpetual darkness behind her.

"Sure thing."

I poured the day's first cup, sloppy in my hand, and then returned, coffee sloshing, to Juliet's room. The day's first coffee attracts chaos; being a good parent hinged on how quickly I responded to Juliet's needs. Spit out words. Smile with an effort ingrained by years of practice at hiding my feelings, hoping Juliet wouldn't detect the tension beneath my disguise. In parenting, as in life, selfishness battled duty; they may as well have been best friends, these enemies who relied on each other for the very fight that defined them.

Wearing this mask (like a therapist, or a priest), I knocked softly, walked in. "What's up?"

I pushed aside Juliet's sketchbook, looseleaf, library books, and half a carrot to sit cross-legged on the floor, coffee steaming. I made a mental note to do the rounds later, collect her dirty laundry with my red plastic hamper. I deferred my nagging, though there was much to nag about, noticing as I adjusted to the pale gloom what lay

4

around me on the grey utility carpet: a salad bowl filled with some kind of semi-opaque liquid and a couple of kitchen pots, all three emitting a sour smell.

I remember the smell. The ivy vine I'd overwatered, killed, and thrown in the garbage a couple of days ago, rescued and now in a paper cup on her windowsill. Juliet's pallor, her face the shade of Jadeite dishes.

She sat down cross-legged on the floor in front of me. Enfolded in an old tracksuit and a baggy, shapeless grey cardigan, fraying, a hole at the elbow. Her hair greasy.

"Is it okay if I miss school tomorrow?"

"It all depends on the why."

Vomit in the bowl, in the pot.

Hangover.

Juliet hungover?

Electricity prickled the hair on the back of my neck. I saw a mini montage of me as a teenager, and before I could launch into a spiel about underage drinking and throwing your life away, Juliet added, "Actually, could I take a few days off?"

"I guess that would depend on . . ."

The vision morphed.

Not hungover. Pregnant.

Morning sickness.

Sixteen and a mom?

We'd work through this. I'd stay home while Juliet finished school. I ran with other scenarios. She may want an abortion. I looked from the bowl to the pots and waited. And then what did I ask? If she was sick? If she was pregnant? No. Instead I smiled to reassure her. *When someone you know is in trouble, shut your mouth and open your arms.*

I removed all judgment from my voice: "What's the deal?"

I'm still reeling from her next words.

"I tried to kill myself," she said.

6   The carpet's industrial weave rasped my legs. I shook my head, muttering, "No, no, no," the floor my only security. I didn't yell, "What the fuck? How could you?" but nor did I scoop her up in my arms and hug her tight and say, "Everything's going to be okay, don't worry, I'm here to look after you." I wanted to be the carpet. I wanted to melt into its fibres.

I tried to kill myself.

Her words repeated in my mind, their import hitting me in the face like the metaphorical slap.

Shock, of course, reset the system. Recoded the body. My cortex tried to take it all in: Juliet's bedroom in October. Two weeks shy of Halloween. Rain and fog beyond the double-hung windows. The two of us sitting on Juliet's carpet. A grey halo around the window blinds. Juliet's loft bed. First cup of coffee of the day in my hand. Evaluate. Make a decision.

Why was this happening?

Did it matter? Why was for later. For now, what was I going to do? Become aware of the ridiculousness of former ordinary things? The coffee mug in my hand, hot, still spinning out steam? Music coming through the ceiling? The pinging of the portable radiator? The hum of the bathroom fan?

I was trapped in the why even as I was yet to establish the when and what and how, yet to assess the severity of Juliet's physical symptoms, yet to decide whether to call 911 or find her a psychologist. Trapped in an apocalypse, in the ancient Greek sense of an unveiling.

A mystery. A thing I didn't understand.

I didn't need to. Because the ascribed importance of what we did, get married, dream, make goals, make love, have children, ignored the make-believe of who we were. What we made ourselves believe in. What was important was how to move, how to get up from the carpet, how to open my mouth and make words come out, how to do this. I could do this.

Coffee swirling, upstairs music wafting down.

To look at my child, this person I'd once carried under my heart, standing at the precipice over a void . . . Any attempt at calm efficiency would be difficult.

"How?" I asked. (How did you try to kill yourself? In despair? In acute pain?) "How?" (Could such an act of violence ever find its roots in logic?)

"I took a bottle of Tylenol. But don't worry, Mom, I puked it all up."

"How much did you take?"

"The whole bottle."

Oh God. "Do you still have it?"

Juliet passed me the Tylenol box, her nails chipped, and the bottle, value-pack size. I shook it, then read the warnings. "When did you take these?"

"Most I took Friday, some Saturday."

It was Sunday now. I reached across her desk, an old hand-painted door on cinder blocks covered with stickers, to grab her laptop. I googled Tylenol overdose and amounts. The computer asked me if I meant *t-y-l-e-n-o-l*; I clicked yes. The first website said Tylenol didn't kill all at once.

"It took a while. I kept gagging. The pills were so sweet," Juliet said.

I tried to understand. I didn't understand. Friday. Saturday. There'd been nothing out of the ordinary then; it made no sense.

In the months to come I will try to parse Juliet's life and my life, detective-like, create order, analyze scraps, give my confusion words, my head like an evidence room stuffed so full of unanswered clues that its door is no longer closing, it groans under its own weight, its floorboards bowing.

"I only told you because it didn't work."

The estimated lethal dose of the drug is ten grams in one day. Liver damage has been described from six grams onward, unless an antidote can be administered in time.

I grabbed a piece of paper to do the math. Fifty thousand milligrams of Tylenol, two days. I took away the zeros. Fifty thousand milligrams equalled fifty grams, right? Thirty-six hours or so. We were still in the safe zone, right? Oh, Lord. We were only now entering the danger zone.

I did not make these findings known to Juliet.

"I puked yesterday morning, and night. And Friday night."

"Friday night?" It was going to be okay because she'd puked. That's what the hospital had people do. Throw up. Or was it feed them charcoal? "How are you feeling? Right now?"

"My stomach hurts a little, but it's not too bad."

When to Seek Medical Care
You must call a doctor, a poison control center, or emergency
medical services for any suspected acetaminophen overdose.

In the Comments section a retired general internist, a former intensive care physician, had written: "It is a terrible way to go. It takes days while your liver totally fails, you feel nauseous, regret your deed, then, if no liver transplant can be done, die miserably."

I learned, to my dismay, that Tylenol, a stealthy warrior, dug in with time, gained force. I learned that Juliet had been wrong about its having failed, and I offered a prayer of thanks for the sole reason that it meant she'd actually told me. In fact, the warrior roaming Juliet's system had been growing stronger. With Tylenol the danger came forty-eight to seventy-two hours after ingestion. Even in a hospital, those who ODed sometimes died.

"It took me so long to get them down. After downing about half the bottle, I nearly gave up."

"I think maybe we should go to the hospital," I said evenly, words that at their heart meant *Where did I go wrong?* Everything I'd believed, hoped for, thought I had, my biggest accomplishment, a daughter, a happy family, a lie.

"Nah. I don't feel like going anywhere. I'd have to take a shower."

I snapped down the computer lid. Juliet's skin had paled to the shade of ear wax. Not wanting to alarm her—did fear make the poison travel faster?—I said, "Let's just go and get you checked out, just to be safe."

"Do I have to?"

If she refused would I throw her over my shoulder kicking and screaming in my ear like a child refusing to leave the playground?

Juliet was a stranger, a green face, still sitting cross-legged in the spot where I'd once had a daughter.

I took a deep breath and feigned calm. "It won't take long. It'll be an adventure. It'll be fine."

She shrugged. Knowing the moment could flip on a dime, while she was putting on her shoes I ran out to the hallway then up the steep stairs to the loft. In the middle of the floor Syd sat on our mattress listening to Deep Purple.

"We need to go to the hospital," I said. I kept my voice steady. "Juliet tried to kill herself."

TWO

12   Syd pulled his coat over his bathrobe. Then we were leaving the house, driving down the road, and I turned to Juliet beside me, resting her head against the window.

"How you feeling?"

"Greasy. This is stupid. Can we go home?"

Syd stared straight ahead.

We approached the hospital's looming big red EMERGENCY sign. Syd stopped in the turnaround outside the automatic doors. "I'll get parking. I'll find you." Juliet and I slid from the truck; for an instant, I imagined Syd dropping us off, pulling a U-ie, driving home, and leaving us stranded there. The automatic doors opened to swallow us like a big mouth.

Hospitals should be a place of light, like the seaside, where one may find healing; instead we moved through the bowels of a beast that breathed from vents and exhaled into rooms Dickensian with suffering. The walls were chipped from stretchers clipping corners at high speeds, brittle with pain. We found the reception area where a sign told us to take a number, like at a deli, and I wanted to reverse time as I went through the motions, settled Juliet in a chair, pulled a paper tongue from the dispenser, lacking words of comfort or counsel as we waited, three people ahead of us, including a man whose injured hand was wrapped in dish towels.

From triage we heard "Catholic beds! Catholic beds ain't good for nothing." And "Goddammit, will one of you bitches help me turn over?" "Do you have a bag? I mean a purse? A bag with a bone." "No, I left mine at home, sweetheart." "I need a phone. My son is looking all around this place right now." "Oh, a phone. That's different from a bone." "Someone get me the fuck out of this Catholic bed! Fort Battleford! C'mon, Wendy! Make her mad!"

It was hard to read Juliet's face amid the ruckus; she wouldn't shed light, offer clues. She used to wear vampire teeth as a fashion statement, clothespins as accessories like coat brooches. I don't mean to suggest these are clues, yet they point to something. I sat uselessly in a chair at her side, squeezing her hand. I told myself that this was for the best, that she'd finally get the help she needed. That she'd stop falling through cracks.

Syd took the empty seat beside me when he arrived, not the one next to Juliet.

I sat in the middle, as always, Syd on one side, Juliet on the other. Syd mumbled about missing breakfast and then said nothing, the strong, silent type. *Shut your mouth and open your arms when someone you love is in trouble.* He stared into space and the silence grew louder—I could write a whole book about disguises—lost in his own struggle to understand, but censure radiated from his stillness, and what he was trying to understand was why I'd made a big deal out of nothing, why I'd taken things too seriously, why I'd been too dramatic. Nothing riled Syd— but nothing touched him, either. And although I hadn't felt any anger, now I turned to him and said, "Would you like something from the vending machine?" as angrily as I could.

Juliet had no appetite, yet it turned out that she hadn't eaten since Friday night, when she'd made us dinner. She did that a couple of times a week, and with our health in mind, things like broccoli, eggplant, chickpeas. She liked health food. Always had.

How had she sat through that Friday night dinner— pork chops that she herself had braised with red peppers, served with basmati rice—while Syd complained about work? How could Juliet have joined us at the table hoping she'd be dead by morning? How had she fooled me?

At what point, exactly, had she taken the pills? When had she had the time? After dinner we'd walked to the gas station, strolled our tree-lined street, the three of us keeping pace with a tourist family, matching blankets around their shoulders, waving at us from the backs of horses, their tails braided with flower garlands.

We'd bought junk food at the station the night the poison travelled through Juliet. We'd rented a movie, a weekend ritual I insisted on to strengthen our family bond. Back at home we'd piled onto the upstairs mattress, still crunchy from last week's crumbs.

Juliet, I learned later, had taken fully half the poison by the time we started the movie. Juliet, dying, had curled herself into the fetal position at my feet.

Halfway through the movie she'd said, "I'm tired. Think I'm going to bed."

"Okay, champ. Have a good sleep," I said, involved in the inane plot.

Now we sat in the waiting room, Juliet's hand cold in mine.

I tried to buy chips from the vending machine but kept pushing "E-E" instead of "EE" and got eight-dollars'-worth of the wrong candy. A man struggled with his

IV pole at the door, glancing my way abjectly; I diverted my gaze toward the white letters on green arrows pointing to other departments down the hall. Signs of what lay ahead.

Why had she wanted to leave me?

I thought I knew my daughter. I'd needed to ask one question at a time, like people in a queue, each as important as the next, nothing overlooked. To ask Juliet *Why?* was the last thing she needed. But I needed to drown out the loop of what she'd told me so far, the words still reverberating in my head like a guitar amp on echo.

Our number was called. I made myself move as if I weren't mid-panic. I told myself not to jump around like a crazy woman. Above all, not to cry.

Juliet told the nurse what time she'd taken the Tylenol, and how much. She was admitted right away, put into a wheelchair, a plastic bracelet fastened around her wrist with her name, her birthdate. There was no judgment. Only speed and concern, a chilling look, frightening efficiency.

I plunged into hell. Juliet closed her eyes, escaping my ineffectual reach, closing herself off from her terrible mother. She looked old, wrapped as she was in a blanket from home, her skin pale green, the same green it had been leaving the house, forgetting to lock the door.

The nurse told us that time was of the essence as she rushed Juliet along a corridor. "Tylenol is one of the worst drugs out there," she said.

three

18   Over the next six hours doctors examined Juliet, all asking the same questions the nurse at admitting had: how much? and when? Now Juliet sat, silent and sullen, on the edge of her hospital bed, rustling the sheets when she moved. She looked vulnerable in her blue gown, her back exposed to her lead doctor—with a boyish face and a soft beard he'd probably grown to make himself look older—listening to her lungs and heart with a stethoscope, forcing me to repeat all the now-familiar answers. Juliet remained silent, as did Syd, as if along for the ride.

How did things work in a hospital anyway? I thought it a careless oversight that information I'd given to the first person couldn't be relayed to the second and the third.

"We've answered this," I said, producing the Tylenol box, "for the others." The doctor took it from my hand, glanced at it, passed it back. Juliet lay back and looked at the ceiling. "Friday," I told him. "Friday evening, and on into Saturday, I believe." I turned to Juliet for help. "The last ones you took . . . ?" She shrugged. I went on: "Saturday, maybe one, two in the morning? Can't you pump her stomach?"

Too late for that, he explained: neither vomiting nor a tube wash would work; the drug had already left the gastrointestinal tract. I imagined a shipful of warriors setting sail, gliding through her bloodstream and ready for battle. Instead, the doctor continued, they'd insert a cannula in her arm to deliver an antidote by IV. The drug he'd be giving her, he said, was N-acetylcysteine. It sounded like A-Settle-Sistine, like the Sistine Chapel, minus the beauty. It would act as a sponge, essentially, giving the acetaminophen something besides Juliet's liver to chew on.

The problem, he said, tapping his pen on his clipboard as if referring to a speed bump on the road, was the time factor. Hepatotoxicity began twenty-four to seventy-two hours after ingestion, enzyme levels continuing to rise for forty-eight to ninety-six hours, even when no more acetaminophen was introduced.

A nurse arrived pushing a medical shopping cart. He turned to Juliet, engaging my quiet, suffering, sleepy

19

daughter in a chat about music as he tried to find a vein. What's your favourite band? Live gigs versus recordings? Vinyl versus digital? To get an IV into Juliet's arm, the IV that would deliver the saving medicine, was proving interminable. He kept pricking, then apologizing, growing more frustrated and flustered by the minute.

"I'm so sorry," Juliet said drowsily.

He palpated her veins. "They're so small," he remarked. "Small and delicate, like you."

He tightened the tourniquet. It looked like one of those resistance bands for home exercise.

By now she'd had multiple jabs and he seemed no closer to success.

"I'm so sorry, gee," Juliet said again. She lowered her head, penitent.

Her glazed eyes reminded me of a child prone to high fevers, in the room but not completely, and I could do nothing to stop the part of her that had already left her body.

"Damn," said the nurse. "Nope. Let's warm you up." He wrapped Juliet's arm in a blanket. "Sometimes if you're too cold your veins don't pop."

Bruises from the cannula appeared on Juliet's waxy skin, from her wrist to her inner elbow. Two of the pricks sprang leaks.

The nurse taped cotton balls over them and then unhooked the walkie-talkie on his belt. "We've got a difficult stick," he said, and received a crackling response I couldn't make out. My mouth was dry, making it hurt to swallow. "The cavalry is on the way," he said. "A vascular specialist."

Syd reached for my hand, and I reached for Juliet's. The three of us, touching, like paper dolls.

The specialist arrived, pushing up his sleeves and then his glasses.

Juliet lay on the bed growing drowsier by the minute, whether from the drugs or the lack of sleep I didn't know. She shrank under the covers, still apologizing for her small veins. I felt a surge of protective anger every time she took responsibility for their delicacy.

Light from the window, from a fluorescent strip above her bed, from squares in the ceiling, oversaturated us and made Juliet's green skin look even greener.

I leaned into Syd the way a fighter leans into his opponent and let the weight of his arm, now around my shoulder, comfort me. Juliet couldn't die. The story of her name was a wish: Juliet and Romeo lasted only three days, but look, people were still talking about her. That girl had dented eternity. Juliet couldn't die, but was. Dying. We were all dying and no one could stop it, as powerless as bare hands trying to prevent fog from rolling over the hills. I pushed Syd's arm away. This was all my fault. I didn't deserve comfort.

Later, the chaplain would assure us that this wasn't our fault. He spoke of God's love shining through the medical professionals, and of God's mercy.

Juliet drew up her heavy lids with difficulty, like the blanket walls of a nomadic encampment, then shut them again.

four

No one died all at once, as no one's birth occurred all at once. Processes required time. Finally the vascular specialist had gotten a vein, set up a drip. Whatever the hospital's visiting policy might be, I refused to leave. It was now two in the morning. Syd had gone home. There was no chair by Juliet's bed; I'd walked all around but couldn't find one I could haul back to her room.

One nurse called me pushy, coldly asking me to move to the other side so that she could administer what needed to be administered. Another ignored me completely. I understood that they had a job to do, but I did too, as a mother, for my baby. I remained at her side, trusting no one.

I spent the first night on the hospital floor. Lying on my stretched-out jacket, using my arm as a pillow, I tried to sleep. Nothing would tear me away, least of all a nurse who didn't tell me to go home yet made it clear I wasn't welcome, as if it wasn't my place to stand vigil. The staff regarded the desperation in my voice with suspicion, looking at me as if I'd become unhinged. As, of course, I had. Juliet wasn't taking life seriously, wasn't taking *her* life seriously. And no one was taking her cry for help seriously but me.

I woke, chilled and stiff, a few hours later. The ward silent, low chatter coming from the nurses' station, which remained lit all night. Monitoring machines ticked and hummed.

Juliet had been placed in a room on a locked ward. I'd been trying to quit smoking but now I caved. With Juliet asleep, I bought a pack from the gas station. I stood across the street from the hospital, whose walls were covered in "No Smoking" signs, in the same pyjamas I'd been wearing when Juliet told me about the overdose. A couple waiting in a bus shelter turned away after meeting my eye. The drag felt as good as a slow caress, a soft consolation, made me feel like I was doing something even though I was doing nothing. Its fragrance calmed my heart a little, my heart the glowing ember, a spot of brightness in the dark. I watched the tobacco dwindle with each drag. I dropped the butt, crushed it under my heel. Afterward I walked on to clear my head, a fast loop around the whole hospital, a breeze drying my lips.

On my return to Juliet's room I noticed something I hadn't earlier. Nowhere—not with her pyjamas in the plastic patient bag, in the bathroom adjoining her room, on the rolling table, in the locking cupboard—nowhere was her Chinese bathing suit. She'd left her lucky talisman. Juliet was someone I no longer knew, capable of anything.

At four years old, hand on her hip, head cocked, pony-tail over one eye, Juliet had announced that she no longer needed daycare. I'd just started the business, then, selling used clothes online, photographing them on a mannequin I'd rescued from the garbage. "Mommy, look at that sad lady," Juliet had said, pointing at a dumpster. We'd needed money a few months earlier and so I'd sold my clothes. One thing I've learned is it *pays* to take care of things well. Photography, not fashion, was my true passion but when I realized how profitable resale was, I turned it into a business. After we'd washed the spaghetti sauce off the torso, Juliet christened her "Betty" and *Betties* became the name of our virtual store.

One should never talk down to one's child, I'd reached for her hands, told her that experts viewed daycare as a key agent in the development of social skills. Besides, I'd said, they have monkey bars.

"Fine. But I want a Chinese bathing suit."

"What's a Chinese bathing suit?"

"They're lucky." She explained that the Olympic divers who won gold medals wore them.

"Deal."

She wore that suit everywhere. It wasn't an exact copy of the one she admired but the discount store had something similar in her size and she never took it off, even to bathe, which spoke to me of a neediness I was unable by temperament to address. In the deal I managed to strike she had to remove it once a week so that I could put it in the washing machine. "If not, I'll take it away." She slept, the bathing suit in her hand, under her cheek, wore it like a pocket handkerchief, her fetish, never left the house without it.

Around midnight of that first night I remembered I'd have to call Juliet's school.

Juliet, who had recently begun grade twelve, was on the honour roll. She had made me proud, considering where we'd come from, excluded for so long by peers who understood their entrance to Queens or McGill was a given.

In elementary school Juliet had been bullied for the thrift-store clothes I dressed her in, until they sold. She protected my feelings by mentioning nothing, and in response to slurs rubbed her bullies' faces in evermore unsightly combinations—mustard cords with raccoon stoles—and wore her thrift-store clothes like a badge of honour. I only found out because a parent reached out to me and said there was a squabble going on, that we needed to bridge this bit of drama.

Although she was skipped a grade, she was less known as the gifted child through elementary and middle school, that age when children can be most cruel, than she was the disrespectful child, the rule breaker, the back talker, the eye roller. Juliet the Mouthy, Juliet the Unreasonable, Juliet the Bitch. She had a sense of justice, was willing to fight for anyone like her who hadn't been given a fair shake, needed her protection, and was suspended a number of times for physical confrontations. She even protected those who didn't want her protection, hadn't asked for it, including me, in a role-reversal that troubled me as much as it made me proud. For instance, grabbing a cigarette straight from my mouth when I was supposed to be quitting and snapping it in half, a behaviour that had amped up after seeing a smoker's lung in school, at which point I'd said, "I'll quit, I'll quit!" and told her I'd do all I could to fight the urge, though in the privacy of my own mind the battle raged. "Are you trying to kill yourself? Do you want to *die*?" she said, and all I could see in her eyes was sadness, a disappointment so deep that I began hiding in the trailer, locking it behind me, the only key tucked in my palm, every time I caved and lit up.

The year before, in grade eleven, Juliet had been awarded a medal for outstanding academic achievement. By then, she'd amassed a following on Instagram for her fashion sense as well as for her art since she'd begun to paint. Friends and strangers commissioned work from her—she had a Tumblr site, and worked hard. Old enough for her first paper route, she rose at five a.m. without complaint, delivering papers on time, rain or snow. Later on: bakery clerk, door-to-door canvasser for a children's aid organization, math tutor—she often worked two jobs at once. Using my store as a platform, she invested in comic books and flipped them online. The principal had phoned to tell me of the honour, and could I please have her in the gym at seven p.m. the following Monday?

The night of her award ceremony, Juliet was still refusing to go.

I'd spent the day posting clothes to my website, dressing my mannequin Betty and taking pictures of her in a fifties car coat and then an angora dress, like the fashion photographer I fancied myself and sometimes told people I was. If I made five or ten dollars on a sale I was happy.

It had never really been about the money. I read an email from a woman who'd purchased a wool cape for her mother's eighty-fifth birthday, writing to thank me because her mother had been thrilled, because the cape had been identical to one stolen from her at twenty, the first time she wore it, walking home from a movie theatre. I forgot to put on oven mitts and checked the slapdash meal of frozen pizza with bare hands. Holding onto the dish for too long, glancing over at Syd, messing about at the dinner table with something requiring a screwdriver and electrician's tape, I knew that to call in his help would be to invite a machine gun to a knife fight, so I didn't run my hands under cold water but rather whispered in Juliet's ear that I'd give her an iTunes gift card if she went. Her compliance representing a tugboat, towing my future behind it.

"On condition that I don't have to dress up," she said.

So Juliet hadn't bothered to dress up. She went in the clothes she'd worn to school that day, a sixties romper I'd posted for thirty dollars because of the stain on the front, and one of Syd's hoodies.

On the way, Juliet still protesting: "Oh my God. Seriously."

By the time we got to the school she was insisting we go home. I remember her slouching across the parking lot. I remember her hair tangled. I remember her

29

shoulders rounded as if within the hollow of her torso she could hide parts of herself.

She dragged her sneakers through the gymnasium where we made our way to the last empty table, covered by a pink tablecloth, a plastic bouquet at its centre. We sat in the audience of teenagers and their parents, grandparents, uncles, aunts, siblings, cousins. A ribbon on the podium. The lights lowered. The audience in business/formal wear. Not to belabour the point but it was a big deal, and Juliet had made such a small one of it.

To be top. Top of the class, top of the school, not in one subject but two, out of a school population of over a thousand.

My eyes teared up as her name was called. Tears of happiness, of accomplishment by proxy, tears that said no matter what a screw-up I'd been as a mom, no matter the many ways Syd had failed as a father, Juliet had come through a winner.

She rose from the seat next to mine and trudged toward the podium. She smiled widely, posed with the school principal and the minor celebrity host MC—it was easy to see this pained her—then she shook the principal's hand, grasping his forearm, leaning in to say something that made him laugh. Bowed slightly to him as well as to the audience. She put up with photos from various angles, grinning from ear to ear, hand on her hip, cocking her

30

head. The grace with which she accepted the medals surprised me and my eyes teared up again. She walked back to her seat holding the medals without looking at them, flashes still popping.

Finally, then, able to hide among the crowd, she sat down and pulled up the hood of her sweatshirt. "Want these?" she said, as if sharing coupons, and let the medals drop onto my lap. Those medals were round as jam jar lids and heavy as a stick of butter. Solid. I still have them.

"Can we go now?"

"No. We will stay as long as we need to, to be polite."

Scholarship track. Any university she wanted.

On track.

We'd explored options. I'd even suggested applying to European universities, whose offers she could then assess, choosing the most prestigious, or lucrative, or life-enhancing.

Did I think—even once—of what Juliet wanted? She'd never countered my proposals, but she'd been unenthusiastic. Researching campuses and faculty lists, reviewing courses, summoned only shrugs and sighs, and what questions she did ask carried an anxiety that stretched her voice taut. An anxiety I'd assumed was only natural.

"You've got to get ready for the real world," I'd said, as if her days thus far had been only a figment of reality, a fantasy.

All I'd wanted to do was make her aware that society had rules for success. The flip side was doable but hard: getting by in this world without a bank account, without an address. (Try to live without a telephone or email, try to live without language. Without contact. Try sleeping during the day and living at night. Try listening to the voices in your head. Try, just try, telling someone that a demon is alive and well inside you. Try telling someone that they have a demon too, and that you can see it, in their left eye.) See what happens. You know?

That's all.

I never wanted to impose my values on her.

32 *I tried to kill myself.*

The words had carved a niche in the contours of time and now hung, suspended. There was no back. Only forward, a ceaseless march, like a line of little toy soldiers, each one falling off the conveyor belt and into a bag destined to end up on a dollar-store shelf.

five

I had to phone the school. Diligent, in operational mode,
I left Juliet asleep, snoring, small in her bed, and found
the phone in a room at the end of the hall: office chairs,
a basket of children's toys, a window through which I
could see other hospital buildings, their roofs, the seagulls gathered upon them. I followed the prompts on the
attendance line and registered Juliet's absence.

That morning I found a recliner and dragged it into
Juliet's room myself. By the afternoon I'd found a blanket.
As the sun set on the red bricks of an adjacent wing it was
hard not to see the decline of the day as a bitter thing.
I was harrowed. Harrowed by sorrow.

At the seventy-two-hour mark, three days of the
pills working their evil magic on Juliet's liver, I paced

the corridor outside her room, looking for her bearded, too-young doctor. I couldn't bother the nurses again. I'd been to their station twice, and had been checking my watch every few minutes since they'd told me he was on his way. I was anxious for him to arrive before Juliet awoke.

I spotted him emerging from the elevator and launched into interrogation mode. Why was Juliet's skin still the colour of limes? What percentage of failed suicides (what an awful phrase, as though not putting oneself to death represented a defeat) tried again in the weeks to follow? The months to follow? The years? What, doctor, was the recidivism rate over the course of a lifetime?

"Can you tell me what we're still doing here? We were told twelve hours, then thirty-six, now it's day three and she's still green. I don't understand."

I stared at the stethoscope slung around his neck— it wasn't the standard kind but something with braiding and gilt ornamentation; it dangled like a scarf.

"Neither do I," he said, "not completely."

"But she's getting better?" As though to reassure myself.

"Her numbers aren't going down in the way we'd like to see. We administer the N-AC, we note progress, we stop the drip, her numbers rise again." At some point he said the words "liver transplant."

I couldn't understand how, having gotten Juliet to the emergency room in time, she wasn't improving. "So give her more. Why can't you wipe the Tylenol from her system?" I imagined the N-AC as a broom sweeping the bad luck away, the maleficent spirits hiding in the crumbs along the baseboards.

"It's not a case of more is better, Mrs. Barrow."

"It's not Barrow. Duncan. She's Barrow but I'm Duncan."

"Mrs. Duncan."

"Rose."

"Rose. We're doing what we can. It's a waiting game. We're going to send her for an ultrasound, run some more tests. We suspect she may have a fatty liver."

"I don't know much about fatty livers, but enough to know that people who have them are usually fat."

"Try not to worry."

"Just answer, has anyone ever died from a Tylenol overdose after treatment?"

He looked at me as if I'd stuck a needle in his eye. "Cases exist. Does it happen often? No. Has treatment improved since those cases were documented? Yes." He paused. "Please," he said then, squeezing my shoulder, "try not to worry. Okay? I know it's hard."

Then he held out his hand in the direction of Juliet's room. "Shall we?"

Juliet had woken up. She was propped on pillows, wearing her plastic vampire teeth that she always carried with her as a fashion statement. I'd long ago given up asking Juliet why because from day one she'd been who she was, theatrical in presentation, emotional in content.

"How are you feeling?" the doctor asked.

"Good," she said, baring her teeth.

"No pain, nothing?" He sat on the edge of her bed, pressed the tip of his fingers into her abdomen.

She flinched a little.

He questioned us both about mental illness, did it run in the family, and as he spoke Juliet searched my face as if for the right thing to say.

The doctor asked her how often she used drugs.

"I smoked a joint once or twice."

We were that kind of mother and daughter. She'd ask if I wanted to go outside to keep her company while she smoked, having taken up the habit she'd fought so long for me to quit. In my guilt, I'd talk with her for hours even as I resented Syd fobbing off his parental responsibility onto me. Once on the back patio, or under the cedar tree sheltered from the drizzle, she'd say she didn't know what to do about a friend's drinking, confess she'd cheated on a boyfriend, share her anxiety that a flood or earthquake would come in the middle of the night and that's why she slept with her shoes on. She asked me to teach her how to sew skate-punk band patches on her leather jacket, and I showed her how to thread dental floss onto the needle for more strength, but so far as I knew, she'd never entered a mosh pit, slamming her body against others, emerging bloodied and bruised, though I liked to imagine the patch on her leather jacket holding fast.

So when the doctor shifted into asking Juliet about triggers—a breakup? a bad grade? school bullying?—and she shook her head at each one, I already knew that none of these had happened. Juliet would surely have told me if they had.

Instead I wanted to tell the doctor about her sleeping too little or too much, her explosive anger, the delusion she once had that her ankles had turned to glass—for days she'd stayed in bed for fear of their breaking, crawling on all fours to the bathroom. I wanted to highlight the cold detachment required to take a bottle of Tylenol (overdose, staggered) and then go about cooking dinner, serving out pork chops, no hint—no hint!—of regret. But a protectiveness welled up within me; I couldn't bring myself to talk about Juliet while she was sitting right there.

He drew a little circle on a notepad. "Who are you close to?" he asked Juliet.

"My mom."

He smiled at me, drew a bull's eye in the circle, and wrote "Mom."

"Who else?"

"That's it."

"This is you, in the centre." He used his pen as a pointer. "Try to think of other family members or friends you can talk to and put them in the circle, starting with people you can talk to about anything."

"My friends, I guess."

He drew a concentric circle and wrote "Friends." He said, "These are circles of intimacy." He passed her the note-pad and pen. "What about your dad? Do you talk to him?"

Juliet rolled her eyes.

"How about you go ahead and put down your father?"

Juliet, the diligent student, did what she was told. She drew a circle, and on this new orbit around her friends wrote "Syd."

My baby. Tubed arms atop white sheets, propped by two pillows. Beyond the window, brick houses, black tile roofs, a seagull. Wet alder trees, grey sky.

"We have two options," the doctor said. "In-patient psychiatric care or counselling. What do you think, Mom?" he asked, turning to me.

"I think in-patient care is the way to go."

"I'm done, you know?" Juliet said suddenly, her voice breaking.

Part of me wanted to retort that she was never done, that it was not for her to decide.

The doctor pointed us in a different direction. "Can you answer a question for me? What made you think suicide was your only option?"

Juliet considered. I held my breath. We waited. We didn't have to wait long. She answered as if she were a colleague offering a pet theory, a pupil answering an exam question. "Genetics?"

"What about your genetics?"

I'd told her the story: how in my final year of elementary school, when I was twelve, I'd taken a First Aid course for babysitters. That same year, my mother had closed the garage door, started the car, and stuffed a flowered pillowcase into the exhaust pipe. When I found her, I used what I'd learned to save her life.

1. Position the patient on her back.
2. Tilt the head to release the airway.
3. Lift the chin in preparation for artificial respiration.
4. Give two breaths.
5. Watch for the chest to rise.

I placed the heel of my hand firmly on my mother's breastbone, put my other hand atop the first, and began compressions. As the moments passed, I started to compose

39

exactly what I was going to tell her when she opened her eyes. Thinking perhaps "I hate you" or "That's not funny," I continued the chest compressions, thrusting, my elbows locked. I began to cry. Then panic took over: I screamed every schoolyard curse I knew. "Fuckhead! Dickwad! Asshole! Bastard!" The words boomeranged off the garage walls. She wasn't responding, yet I clung to hope the way a mountaineer clings to a rope.

After fifteen minutes I realized I'd made the biggest mistake of all. Forgotten the most important thing they'd drilled into us during our class, an omission for which I could never be forgiven. I'd neglected to call an ambulance, which I did next. Three decades on, I still believe the delay is what killed her.

My father arrived shortly after the ambulance crew. A few hours later the police gave us a shoebox they'd found in the trunk of the car. A Harry Belafonte tape, a wedding band, a to-do list, houseplant watering instructions.

Who would wash my gym clothes? Who would make dinner? In the ensuing days and weeks my father would go straight to bed after work. Or he'd go to the bar. One night he didn't bother coming home at all. I taught myself to cook.

What follows is banal. My father met a woman who was to become my stepmother and we moved to a city on the coast. I sucked in my feelings as one sucks in an unsightly bulge, and my father—who wasn't a bad man, just unseeing—praised my bravery.

I didn't have to wonder what harmful things I'd burdened Juliet with, what she was sucking in because of me. I could list them. And I expected her to list them herself, now that the doctor had asked the million-dollar question.

"Why did I want to die? I was too happy."

The answer flabbergasted me.

If the doctor was surprised, he hid it well. "That's unusual. Most happy people don't want to end their lives."

Juliet was done talking. She turned away, taking the plastic teeth out of her mouth and laying them on the side table like a pair of dentures.

"Your homework," he said to her back, "is to think of more names. And maybe about talking to your father."

I followed him out of the room, into the hallway, tile floors and open doors, each leading to some other family's grief. Now that we were out of Juliet's earshot, I told him about Syd leaving in the bathroom his opioid prescription for pain after a motorbike accident. About the fentanyl patches we'd once found in her bedroom; she claimed a friend had used them. Isolated incidents, but still. I tried to highlight Juliet's cold regard for her own beating heart. "She said nothing. Do you understand? She swallowed an overdose and then calmly made us dinner. Too happy? What does that even mean?"

41

I'd been telling doctors for years that Juliet was clinically depressed. No one, I felt, had taken me seriously. And now here was unassailable *proof* and still I wasn't being taken seriously.

And this doctor . . . I was cross. How could he be listening if he kept looking at his watch?

When had I last eaten? he asked, putting his hand on my shoulder. "It's important for everyone in the family to look after their health." He asked if I was in therapy, if I had anyone to talk to.

Then, before I could say another word, he disappeared into an elevator down the hall.

42

six

I phoned my friend Ron. A retired movie stuntman, he had a wife and son who lived in India. He saw them once a year and fished on a tuna boat the rest of the time, more for the pleasure of being on the ocean than the money. I marvelled at their strange relationship—they'd never lived together. But she'd never divorced him, either.

"Can you imagine what kind of man he must be?" I asked Syd one night in bed.

"The asshole kind?"

"I don't think so. He must really have something to keep her married to him."

"Money."

I lay awake listening to Syd's snores, tracing my fingers over my stomach and imagining the carnality of Ron and his wife who packed their pleasure into a single month each year. Maybe using the Kama Sutra.

What else can I tell you about Ron and the way he helped me in those weeks and months following Juliet's suicide attempt? Ron had known Juliet since she was born. A trail through the forest connected his house to ours and Juliet would often toddle over, making a beeline straight for his vegetable garden. She'd sit among the rows to pluck fresh peas from the vine and look for bright red strawberries hidden under the leaves.

Juliet with a long hollyhock as a fairy wand. Juliet sling-shotting raccoons in hallways of trees. Climbing onto the shed roof and pulling all the tiles off. Cooking her pet turtle and throwing the shell over our fence.

Ron found it one day while he was weeding his garden. She told us it had escaped.

At the time I was earning extra money photographing used cars for a buy-and-sell newspaper. Sometimes I'd take Juliet with me, but Ron was always a willing babysitter if I knew a job would have me driving home from an address late. He and Juliet would pick up some of her friends and he'd entertain them all at his house—antics, more fresh strawberries, and sometimes even slow rides on the back of an old Clydesdale he kept in a paddock.

"Kids will be kids," he said.

"I've never seen a five-year-old so full of rage."

"Maybe she's holding onto something from a past life."

"What do I tell Syd?"

"The truth."

But when I finally screwed up the nerve to tell Syd, he didn't react the way I'd anticipated. Instead of being furious—Syd like a light-switch that can flip instantly—he downplayed the event. His gut told him I was over-reacting, but his gut just wanted something to believe in.

I wondered out loud whether Juliet's need to shock was a mask to hide how small she felt inside. Syd said that didn't change the meaning of right and wrong.

But if Syd was the stern hand of reason, then Ron was the fun-loving uncle. This is why children loved Ron, and sometimes I dreamed he'd taken Syd's place as the family head, the way an understudy takes on the leading role if the star gets sick. Syd, sick of work, sick of his boss, sick of traffic. And certainly sick of my complaining about how Juliet scribbled in her notebook, blasted the music, painted for hours, disguising something she needed professional help with in a cloak of darkness. He never saw her behaviour through the same lens as I did. "You just want to deliver her to the altar of psychiatry saying, Fix her. That's our job," he said. He pressed his lips together; he'd never hidden his opinion of mental health workers.

"What are you so afraid of?"

It's not that golden moments didn't exist between Syd, Juliet, and me—I could fill a book with them. At Christmas he'd dress as Santa and ring bells outside her window; she thought Santa's sleigh was landing and would rush to the kitchen to fill a cereal bowl with water and another with carrots, setting both on the front step. "For the reindeer," she'd say. Juliet believed in Santa until she was twelve.

But perhaps a small part of me thought she deserved more. So maybe I could be forgiven for, lately, calling back that same familiar old fantasy that had hung around like an old velvet dress in the closet, rarely worn, but too precious to sell: that Ron would look after me.

Ron proved himself reliable, in sickness and in health, although no rulebook said he needed to; he'd taken no vows. Syd, the kind of man who judged people by the quality of their dogs, trusted Ron too.

I told Ron about Juliet's reason for what she'd done. "Too happy," I said. "I told her I understood—that it was like leaving a party in full swing. Not waiting for the empties and hangovers, you know? Daylight."

He nodded. "It sounds familiar. Suicide-at-Moment-of-Greatest-Happiness. Like some kind of Japanese thing."

seven

Juliet had been "sectioned" in a ward and was under twenty-four-hour surveillance. The doctor told me I could go home, that he'd make sure she wouldn't try to kill herself again. I wanted to shout, How long between your periodic checks would it take a person to escape the ward and slice their aorta? To jump out a window?

When Juliet headed to her bathroom, I followed her in.

"Mom."

"What?"

"Mom? I'm peeing."

I nodded.

"Geez, Mom."

Later I followed her back to bed.

It was never really what you were going through that counted, but rather how you thought about it: your sense of things, and whether you believed—whether you still hoped—you'd make it through the night.

eight

The following day, in the tiny sunroom at the end of the
hall in that hospital ward, its warmth intensifying my
exhaustion, I called Juliet's principal.

He asked me how long I thought Juliet would remain
absent.

"I don't know. We're waiting on her numbers."

"If it's longer than a couple of weeks, we'll have to
make arrangements."

He'd arrange private lab times. He'd arrange for
Juliet to come in only once a week, if that was all she felt
comfortable with.

"I suppose she can always graduate a year behind,"
I said, thinking out loud.

"What helps the recovery process, I've found, is to *not* let them pull back. Involvement—not isolation—is the key to recovery."

"You're saying that Juliet . . . shouldn't take any time off?"

"It's something you'll have to think about when she comes home from the hospital." He admired Juliet's potential, her intelligence, that much was clear. He acted like a person in possession of a treasure, a jewel in the hand, a small bird that needed to be coddled. "I just want to share with you that I've had to deal with one or two attempts a year. I've had a little experience."

We made an appointment to discuss the matter a few weeks down the road, when Juliet was feeling up to it.

That afternoon Juliet had a friend, a classmate I'd known since he was a little boy, visit her. His name was Aleeki. I'd texted him, peppered him with questions: "Did you know? Did you have any clue? Could you feel something like this coming on?"

"No," he'd said. "I'm shocked. This came without warning. I had no idea."

A couple of months before, in the waning days of summer, the three of us had gone to the beach for the day, packing a lunch, bringing our towels. Juliet went for a swim and later, emerging from the water (her flesh goosepimply, drying off with a towel, droplets of ocean dripping from her limbs onto the sand, stones beneath our heels), revealed consecutive razor cuts marking both thighs. Aleeki, alarmed, asked what the marks were from. The edges, exposed to moisture, appeared grey and soggy and soft. Juliet, who'd always been interested in art, in painting, in the history, its traditions, had answered calmly.

"I'm painting in blood these days. It's all for the art."

Never wanting to discourage her artistic tendencies, believing in her visceral commitment to process, I'd refrained from judgment. I offered a suggestion: "Maybe next time we can go to a butcher and ask for some blood. You don't need to use your own."

Seriously? Teenage angst on a canvas? Why hadn't I pursued it with her? How had I not seen it as a cry for help?

"Yeah," Aleeki had said. "That looks pretty nasty."

I had proudly displayed a blood painting on the mantel, but somehow, after a month of its being there, I hadn't noticed when it went missing.

Now I'd begun combing through Juliet's social media posts to discover red flags, if any, I'd missed— such as Juliet giving things away on Facebook. She'd made the offer public: "If you want a painting, get one.

51

I'm getting rid of all my art." Classic. Many of her friends had responded, none finding her generosity unusual. Juliet must have shuffled her artwork out of the house piecemeal, one painting here, another one there, paintings from art class, laboured over in her bedroom, K-pop playing, her door shut.

I looked at anime posts, art posts, food photos, party photos, silly grins, beers raised like torches, joints hanging out of mouths, the trading of memes, the trading of music, posts going back months. Then I saw a text Juliet had sent me the day before we went to the hospital, eighteen hours after she'd taken her final dose of Tylenol: "Mommy, can you come see me?" And then, a few minutes later, "Plllleease?" Messages she'd sent me from her bedroom and messages I wouldn't receive until now. Juliet hadn't called me "mommy" since she was a toddler. It broke my heart. But there was nothing that could help me figure out at what point Juliet had moved from someone living to someone who wanted to throw the best gift we had in the garbage. Nothing to help me understand.

At the age of three, around the same time she stopped calling me mommy, she said kisses were for sissies and that she no longer wanted any. I said, "Okay. You let me know when that changes." For two full years I never gave my daughter a kiss, wanting to respect her will, her volition, give her the sense that she could change things, control things, even if in just a small part of her world. Syd, on the other hand, found the request ridiculous, insisted on kissing her whenever he felt like it, against her protests. I should have done the same. Maybe when a three-year-old tells you they don't want your love it's a way of throwing the ball into your court, a way for you to prove that no matter what they said your love was there, as constant as a mountain. Maybe I should have been like Syd, immovable. When my three-year-old said, "I don't want your love," maybe I should have said, "You don't get to choose whether and how I love you. You can fight me, but I'll never let you forget how precious you are to me." Instead I let it go as easily as a wisp of smoke I knew I could never catch in my hand even if I tried.

Now Juliet, Aleeki, and I were taking a few loops around the ward, Juliet pushing her IV bag, her old grey cardigan draped over her cloud-coloured hospital gown. As we waited for the elevator, I was still trying to convey some sense of normalcy. I should have felt at least a measure of relief—Juliet was strong enough to get out of bed—but instead I just felt awkward, and struggled with small talk. You'd think an attempt to take one's own life would have catalyzed the desire for deep discussion, a reflection on what had gone wrong, on what we could do better. On the meaning of life, and of death. On how we all loved each other. None of that happened. We took the elevator to the ground floor and stepped out into the lobby.

The three of us ambled like old women past a man who played piano in the glassed-in sunshine, his thin wrists emerging from the sleeves of his sports coat, the notes of a Strauss-ish piece building and resonating in the fishbowl of light. Bar after bar, his music hammered the dike holding back my sorrow. God seemed to be saying, It's okay. Cry. But who knew what would happen if those dikes broke? To ward him off (a moth to flame, not able to pull away) I said, "He's really good," hiccupping the last word.

Blinking away tears, I turned toward the gift shop that ran down the corridor, gazing through its window: aspirin, chocolate bars, books, mints, water bottles, pillowcases, hand-knitted hats, scarves, tea cozies, mittens, baby booties, slippers donated by the Women's Auxiliary. Each note (a flourish in his wrists) tunnelled in, made cutbacks just as Juliet's thin grey hospital-issue socks with non-slip happy face treads did. Happy Socks.

We waited in line with other red-eyed customers at the bakery, surveying its coffees, its sandwiches behind

54

glass, its lemon squares, almond croissants, gluten-free granola. A glance, the barista's eyes an unlikely transparent blue, streaming as if with sunshine.

"This sandwich is so gross," Aleeki said once we'd settled ourselves back out in the lobby. "I can't eat it."

"You could just kill yourself," Juliet said.

We all laughed. Keep moving. Don't give up.

Then the music ended. "If you were dead," I joked, you couldn't do this." I burst into applause and started the wave.

"Or this." Aleeki, embarrassed, joined in.

Juliet guffawed. "Why would I want to?"

The pianist tipped an imaginary hat, picked up a canvas shopping bag at his feet, and went out the automatic doors, leaving the lobby silent, the only sound now coming from a TV, the talk-show host showing us photographs of a house, then children, then an oversized cheque for a hundred thousand dollars. The TV audience clapped. "I'm *so* glad I'm not dead," Juliet said. "Otherwise I'd be missing this."

55

nine

The walk had exhausted Juliet and she fell asleep as soon as her head hit the pillow. Her room looked as though we'd moved in. Magazines and candy wrappers from the vending machine covered the surface of the sliding table.

There was no "Care of Suicidal Teens" instructional booklet in the hospital library. My gut told me to let Juliet guide the way; her principal had told me the opposite. Ron offered advice along with lasagna.

I'd not been home. I worried constantly that Juliet would reattempt. As long as I stayed she couldn't sneak past the nurses' station with her IV pole, leave with visitors, catch the elevator, exit into the unattended hospital grounds. A short walk to the street. Into traffic.

In the courtyard, birds flew and a steady breeze shook the leaves.

In the dream world you could die and be reborn. I dreamed I'd just given birth. Juliet a few hours old and fussing. "In my country," a nurse told me, "when a newborn cries the old women say she's dreaming of her severed umbilical cord."

A diver's cord is called an umbilical. It delivers a life-saving gas and if it becomes wrapped around anything the outcome could be fatal. A life line is a rope thrown to someone who is drowning by someone on dry ground.

"Yes," I said to the nurse. "Dreaming of something lost."

57

ten

58   Was it because I wanted to make her bear part of my
anguish that I said, "Juliet, your numbers are still not
where they should be," or did I just want to know what
side she was on?

The doctor had left. Juliet was in bed, and as I leaned
over her, seated in my hard-won recliner, she slipped the
arm without the cannula into mine.

"Imagine a cherry tree," she said.

"Cherry?"

"Plum, cherry, whatever. So this tree's blooming.
I mean, it's *covered* in blooms."

I closed my eyes and imagined a bulbous branch,
warm, sweet petal balls. I saw sunshine, the tree, the soil
upon which it stood.

"There's all these cherries. Big ones, little ones, medium ones . . ."

"For pie."

"Everyone expects me to have cherries."

"Is that all?" I opened my eyes and turned to her.

"Honey, you can't help but be full of cherries. It's natural for you. You don't even have to try." She looked confused. "You know? Like our hypothetical cherry tree. It's full of cherries by virtue of its cherryhood, its nature."

"Yeah, but that's the problem."

"That you have too many cherries?"

Symbolic language failing her, she shook her head.

"Okay. Then let's talk about you, not cherries." I realized that an answer was being revealed to me. That Juliet was trying to tell me why she had done what she'd done. But the moment pulled away from my hands and was gone.

She sighed. "You don't get it."

"Try me. Try me again."

She shook her head. "Nah. Forget it." Her voice was not unkind.

Movement outside her window caught my eye. Seagulls had landed on the roof; sparrows, circling the periphery, touched down the briefest of seconds, then flew away. A *seee-seee-seeee* and the caw of crows. Each sound expanded the absence of words between us:

59

at these moments, language, all its nuance and lineage, not as precise as a hospital cart's rattle, laughter spiking down the hall, the ticking wall clock.

In the end, Juliet was to get better. In three weeks' time her numbers were to come down, and talk of a transplant turned into talk of babying her liver, avoiding alcohol, sushi.

Suddenly, Juliet was coming home.

eleven

The doctor had brought a bunch of papers with him. Juliet would be released the next day; the "A-Settle-Sistine," the Tylenol antidote, had finally begun working. She sat on her bed, playing with the little packs of sugar that had come with her breakfast.

"This contract between you and your parents is important," the doctor said. "It means you agree to talk to them if anything's up."

"Okay." Juliet put down the sugar, imitating someone who was paying attention.

He looked at me. "And it means you can ask Juliet how she's feeling and expect an honest answer. Can we do that?" He looked from me to her.

"Yup."

My fist tightened, nails digging into my palm. Juliet's capacity to hide her feelings made the contract meaningless.

"We need to work from a place of trust. Juliet, can your mom trust you to keep yourself safe?"

"Yes," she said.

"Mom?"

I nodded.

"And you'll tell your mom if that feeling changes?"

"Yes," Juliet said again, smiling.

"So. Mom, we have three feelings. Red, yellow, and green. When you ask Juliet how she's feeling, green means I'm great, yellow means I'm not so great, and red means I'm in trouble. Juliet, does that sound good?"

"Sounds good. Thank you, doctor," she added politely.

I peered over my glasses, gave him the evil eye. I didn't feel grateful—I felt dismissed. It felt as if Juliet had been given up on—that I was the mother of a terminally ill patient who'd been told to take her daughter home to die. I'd spent so many days in hallways and in Juliet's room and in cafeterias, walking aimlessly back and forth, that her imminent discharge had come as a surprise blow.

I followed the doctor out into the busy corridor, arms swinging and ready for battle.

"She's troubled," I said, taking off my glasses. "Depressed, and the safest place for her to be is in an in-patient program." I'd been arguing for this since the beginning.

"She doesn't sound depressed to me," the doctor said, squaring his shoulders and straightening his back. "She seems stable enough."

"Stable? What stable person tries to kill herself?" I thrust the arm of my glasses toward him. "No one has even recommended antidepressants."

"She hasn't indicated that she wants in-patient help, and she needs to be a part of her therapy—just as she is in her program."

He'd signed her up for Project Life, an outpatient program at the hospital. Juliet had already attended her first session, an underwhelming experience from the sounds of it.

I was not going to let this go.

"How can you leave it up to a sixteen-year-old? Who's proven she's sick? Isn't trying to kill oneself a kind of insanity? Or at least a response to a kind of insanity? Her liver may have recovered; what about her mind? Can't I, as her parent, make the decisions?"

"At Juliet's age, she has a say. And I don't think she has an issue that would respond to antidepressants."

"Really."

"Look, it's the law. It's called the Mental Health Act. I'm really, really sorry." He crossed his arms, gripping his biceps.

"She's *sixteen*."

"Exactly. If Juliet had come into the hospital at, say, fifteen years of age—"

I was angry, my cheeks burning. "So if Juliet had tried to kill herself when she was fifteen . . ." I couldn't fathom the arbitrary nature of these "laws" the doctor continued trying to explain.

Part of him must have felt bad too. His hands—he was trying to show me, wringing them as he spoke—were tied. In fact, his knuckles were turning white.

"If Juliet needed a blood transfusion," I persisted, "you would ask me, as her mother. So how is this any different? And no one, I repeat, no one knows her child like her mother. Juliet must get the help she needs. I'll get it for her, with or without you. I know you think I'm domineering and I know you dislike me for trying to get Juliet the help she deserves. I'll go to the media," I said wildly. "I'll expose these laws that demand she has the freedom to take her own life!"

Part of my anger stemmed from Juliet's decision to wait a month after her sixteenth birthday. I suspected she'd researched this act. Or maybe not—I had no doubt that she'd counted on death. I understood that the will to survive needed to come from her, but how was that not too tall an order? In any case, I argued for nothing. The doctor's mind was made up, closed to my pleas. He told me again that there was nothing he could do. Then his body pointed, arrow-like, toward the elevator and he scuffled away, his hands in the pockets of his white coat.

The Project Life counsellor, a woman with deep-set eyes and many rings on her fingers, had made the group of troubled teens work at a table with fruit plates. They had been told to track their moods, give them names, draw pictures representing anger and sadness. They were learning mindfulness, emotional regulation, and how to recognize the signs of depression in their body. Juliet had barely taken part. She'd duly attended, yet offered nothing, sitting in near silence until the counsellor gave up.

65

The sessions were private. I knew what I knew through the counsellor, and then only indirectly, as when the counsellor said, exiting the "safe space," "Juliet can go back to her room now."

I'd looked at my watch; a mere ten minutes had passed. "That quickly?"

"She doesn't have much to talk about," the counsellor replied. She sighed, looking like anyone who was overworked and underpaid on the frontlines of the social welfare system.

She reported that Juliet had told her she was fine. When I knew, of course, that she was not. Mostly I failed to understand why the counsellor hadn't dug past "How are you?" Wasn't that her *job*? "How much experience do you have? I mean, I understand huge caseloads, but maybe your training is just inadequate for Juliet's complex problems."

I'd been trying to find out what had precipitated Juliet's overdose. The counsellor returned my gaze with a blank stare. After a moment, she said, "Even the most effective therapist can't *force* people to talk, let alone a silent and uncommunicative teen." And Juliet, for her part, had said simply, "I'm a teenager. Teenagers live in turmoil," as though this sort of thing happened to families every day.

That morning before the day of Juliet's release, I opened her journal while she showered—a violation, and I ought to have respected her privacy, even though someone smarter than I had once conceded that desperate times call for desperate measures. But all the pages were empty.

I hadn't been home since Juliet had been admitted. Syd had continued going to work at the shipyard, visiting when he could in the evenings. I'd asked him to bring me clean clothes. I used Juliet's shower. Syd brought us toothbrushes, Juliet's laptop, a pile of anime books. Now, though, I decided to get her bedroom ready. To make sure her environment would be warm and comfortable.

Worried as I'd been about Juliet, I'd barely registered Syd's comings and goings. Except one night, I remember him sitting beside Juliet at the edge of her bed, leaning toward me, his hand on his cheek, pointing.

"Look at that," he'd said.

"Look at what?"

"Right there." He was pointing at a tiny mark visible only upon close inspection. "That happened while I was at work," he said, and waited.

Expecting sympathy?

I didn't know. I felt a mental kind of nausea, but also a connection between Juliet and me. When our gazes met, I knew we were both thinking, What the hell?

twelve

We were building a respectable, blue-collar home next to an old wooden fisher's cabin at the end of a dirt road, waist-high in mustard weed. The cabin was small, rustic, amply stocked with flannel blankets and tinned beans. The clothes we didn't wear often but couldn't donate to a thrift store for one sentimental reason or another had ended up here. As had old sets of dishes moved when new styles took their place, as well as gadgets we'd bought and whose cost made us feel too guilty to throw out. Our neighbours, Ron included, would visit on the cabin's porch, to share beers, discuss firewood or the best way to field dress a deer, and ogle our firearms—firearms I'd purchased at various gun shows on Syd's behalf but registered in my name because of a ban on owning weapons for a crime

committed when he was a teen—with low whistles of
admiration. Knowing the roots of the crime, it didn't feel,
at the time, irresponsible at all. Both of us had grown up
hunting, and shared its enjoyment as a pastime.

Every job had a halfway point from where you couldn't
see how much you'd done, only the tremendous amount
of work left to do. The newer home next to the cabin,
completed to lock up, had running water and electricity
but no proper carpets, just a shag rug in the centre of a
warehouse-style front room and a subfloor stained now
from years of use. There were no cabinets, and several
of the windows were boarded over. The loft where Syd
and I slept was accessible only by a narrow, ladder-like
staircase. Partitioned from the main room, down what we
referred to as the "hallway" was Juliet's room. Juliet had
painted her room black: black walls, black curtains, black
sheets. She needed things like that—monotone, womb-
like, and simple.

Those windows not boarded over were only temporary—at least, that was the plan. The home stood as a
testament to lost causes and Juliet's illness; for years,
whenever we'd had enough time or money to finish
construction, something would happen with Juliet.

The Anglican church (a little white clapboard building in a stand of alders, surrounded by purple calendulas, whose picturesque graveyard overlooked the ocean)

69

shared a name with the cheapest motel in town. A broken, graffiti-covered sign read "New Beginnings." Summers, the population grew from one thousand to ten thousand. "Weekenders" from the city visited their second (and third) homes; travellers spilled from tour buses; international backpackers hitchhiked clutching Lonely Planet guides. They descended like locusts. They canned tomatoes. Gathered blackberries in a plastic bag. Explored abandoned cabins, collecting things, going room to room, stepping over termite-eaten boards, rat droppings. They treated their treasure hunts as holy and moved in silence, deference. They tiptoed and they took, like missionaries for whom nothing was stealing: photographs yellowing on a mantel, a set of vintage badminton racquets, brass knuckles, the frame of an old iron bed. The elements would have destroyed these objects otherwise, they told themselves; they were protecting, not picking apart, the past.

Invariably Juliet would meet someone from the big city, and true to her namesake she'd go all in, every time, for love. She'd obsess, believing each person she had sex with was The One who would spell the start of a brand-new life, who would save her—and maybe love could have saved her (if she'd fallen in love with the right person, maybe someone from town)—but summer always ended with rejection and heartbreak and the prospect of waiting another six months until she could find a true love to quell the ache. Her fear—taunted, toyed with, and challenged—was that what she needed didn't exist, and that those who left her broken only confirmed that the love of romance novels could not be found in its undiluted form in the real world. Syd talked to her. I talked to her. Nothing worked to diminish the growing cancer in her mind. Her friends still considered her fun to be around. She was fun at parties, fun to dance with, only she'd get into her funks, funks her friends took less seriously as time wore on: they'd heard it all before. By the end of grade eleven she'd gone from brooding to shouting or raging, like a person who'd been burned, constantly thinking of the rip-off, unable to put it behind her. When Juliet was born, Syd and I had both liked the name, having forgotten how tragically the story ended.

As a child, Juliet had attended block parties with barrels of lemonade and kettles of hotdogs. The place was as big or small as your mind: the winding roads (two streetlights at the bridge and two at the grocery store), fetes at church and Halloween hotdogs for the kids (friendly, familiar faces turning up, creating their own importance day after day), potluck dinners and bottles of blackberry wine, handcrafted garden gnomes for sale, local talent (including a whistling concerto at the hundred-year-old Agriculture Hall). But even in paradise people complained, though softly, about leaf blowers before ten a.m., and the gas station always had a petition of some sort on the counter. Retirees yelled all week at apolitical potheads. Housewives, drunk and bored, whacked diaper-bummed toddlers across the ripped seats of pickups (*an ill-fated affair, a suicide*). Bottles of cheap red wine day after day.

Erroneously referred to as "The Cape" at the mouth of the river, our small seaside town was a peninsula, bordered by water, connected to the mainland. Summers it grew, winters it shrank.

The summer before, soaring temperatures had killed mussels, clams, barnacles, sea snails, and starfish for miles up the coast. Cherries cooked on their branches; leaves turned to paper overnight, dropping straight from the trees; tourists carried electric fans. And after the heat came the fire, scattering dust and ash, leaving grapes tasting of smoke in the vineyards, melting cars to their shells, burning houses to their wooden skeletons with only their brick chimneys standing, scorch-marked, as we stood with bottles of water for the firefighters, and it seemed as though the world was coming to an end.

A short, bright fall heralding winter storms arrived as summer faded, gales that smacked us between the eyes, sweeping away whatever the tourists had remained. This was the time of year Syd had begun a tradition of scattering flowers into the ocean to mark the date he'd killed a man.

Experience had taught me that literal distance was just one kind of measure, leaving psychological distance to reckon with. I was often lonely. Then the migraines would start, slow and steady. Why had *that* day, why had any day, been the one Juliet chose? Perhaps sadness had simply caved under its own weight. Not everything had an answer. My head spun. The cape put off my city friends, people who'd drive an hour to visit a pal but wouldn't get on a ferry boat or even cross a bridge, citing the wait, the traffic, the hassle, the cost. In the past I'd invited friends for the weekend who'd said yes at first and then changed their minds.

When I'd moved in with Syd, each box I packed was a goodbye. Each box I unpacked was a loss.

Our road serviced only local traffic or the lost; the lost turned around, forced to return to where they'd come from. As was often said about those who lose their way, it was the panic that killed them, and it irritated Syd, who put up a "No Turnaround" sign; I told him it was easy, to get lost that is. I didn't see them as lost. I'd tried it myself, turned off my headlights and raced down the road at night to induce loss and the true freedom of existing within it; the dead centre of blackness could tell you a lot about yourself. I drove the loop—unimaginatively named Circle Road—that lassoed the cape in its ten-mile circumference off the main road, smaller roads like ours herringboning from it. The thing about a circle was its emptiness in the middle, full of both itself and of nothing at all.

Tourists often drove down our street looking for roadside egg stands, or a store selling clothes that featured pastel butterflies, or a Chinese restaurant, or the nearby dock that jutted into the strait, or the historic trestle bridge where we could go fishing for our dinner.

From a distance, with its wires and girders, the bridge resembled the internal structure of some great animal, maybe the triangular bonework of a dinosaur, feet planted firmly in the water, dorsal fin soaring skyward.

I would stop in the middle of the bridge where the water was the deepest. I liked to take photographs and there was much to capture that was picturesque, apart from the fjord itself, its cliffs and conifers growing along the edge, an overhang of boughs like skirts with bright green trim. Mountains lanced the sky above; scarves of fog embraced the valley below. In the water were kite-surfers, kayakers, sailboats—but what I liked best were the birds. Seagulls, eagles, kingfishers, oystercatchers, cormorants, herons, sandpipers.

The challenge of capturing a bird's flight on film pointed to the difficulty of freezing time in general, the unique angle of the wing gone in a flash.

I'd watch young parents on the beach below the cliffs, toddlers poking at the water's edge with sticks.

But birds were still closer to heaven than children—
Leonardo da Vinci had studied birds—birds could move
up, down, backward, forward, but people were tethered
to the ground—even in an airplane their feet were still
bound to the floor. To get closer to a bird's ineffable sense
of liberty people would take away the very thing most
emblematic of it: their ability to soar.

I wanted to seize their grace, preserve their love of
flying; I could take bird pictures anywhere, but I'd always
felt a magnetic attraction to bridges—when you leaned
over the railing, wind in your hair, you felt as if you were
flying yourself.

I'd never taken a flight, lacking the means, though
float planes serviced the cape and frequently criss-crossed
the sky. We'd kept a jar to fund a vacation but one crisis
or another claimed the money before we ever had the
chance to go anywhere. Every now and then a floatplane
crashed. An accident the year before, the latest but certainly not the last, had made a boom heard on many parts
of the cape, including at our house; Syd, who'd been
clearing stumps, and Juliet and I jumped into his truck
in the direction of the spire of smoke about a half-mile
away. We'd arrived shortly before the first emergency
crews did, and discovered that the plane had sheared the
tops off towering pines, narrowly missed the roof of a
house, and come to rest entangled in brush at the bottom

75

of a valley, a boggy place of wild mint and cattail and deerfoot. Ron pulled up then in his truck. We helped the shaken passengers—miraculously unharmed—and led them to safety, waiting with them until first responders took over.

"Still want to fly?" Syd said to me.

"Your chances of getting hit by lightning are greater than being in a plane crash," I intoned.

"You mean a car accident," Juliet put in.

"No, I think it's lightning."

"No, that's getting married," Ron said. "Your chances of getting hit by lightning are greater than your chances of getting married after forty."

Ron winked at me. I'd racked my brain trying to figure out that wink. For a hundred years the bridge had carried loads across its back, and as such its beauty lay in its duty to others as much as it stood as a monument to humanity. "To fly in the face of" struck me as the perfect expression for bridges and airplanes, human defiance of gravity, ambition in the face of the divine. We built bridges to support connections, as a "fuck you" to God for giving only birds and angels wings.

thirteen

After sleeping in the hospital for those three weeks I was feeling justifiably exhausted. We always manage to cast ourselves, at least those semi-successful at life, as the stars of our own movie. The righteous. The beloved. The brave. Trying to improve my appearance, I turned on the water while Juliet sat on her hospital bed and (though the water was still cold) ran wet hands through my hair hanging from my head with all the limpness of a lost cause.

I pushed open the front door feeling like a stranger, or someone who'd gone on a long trip, coming back to a place they knew was home but that felt different somehow. Of course, it wasn't the house that had changed. It was me.

Even if I didn't know exactly what had altered, I was aware that a shifting had taken place, a rumble. Parts of myself had rearranged themselves, but what they were rearranging themselves into, I didn't know.

I hung my coat on the hook by the door. "Hey," I yelled.

No answer.

Syd was at home: I knew he was home. I heard the music through the ceiling.

He hadn't come downstairs to greet me. Another thing I'd need to think about when I had the mental space, when I had the time. Not now, though. First things first. Juliet's Welcome Back. I needed to scrub her room, raise the blinds.

It would have to wait. The dishes in the sink stopped me in my tracks. Dishes on the counters, fermenting milk glasses, empty boxes of KD, ketchup-encrusted plates on the table. Dirty frying pans on the stove, smudged bar towels, half-finished coffees with floating cigarette butts atop a week's worth of baking pans and colanders. Drinking glasses and squashed lime slices lying where Syd had left them, sticky on the placemats, fruit fly calling cards. Right, I thought, nice, seeing he'd been partying, drinking without me, or more specifically, waiting until I was not around so I wouldn't call him out; and his childish behaviour, his mouse behaviour, at this time, no less, disgusted me.

As I said, the righteous. The beloved. The brave (house keys in hand, still wearing my boots).

I went up the loft stairs. Syd was so quiet on the mattress, peering into his laptop, that I looked over his shoulder, thinking he was looking at porn or talking to another woman. I saw: "Munchausen Syndrome by Proxy."

Before I could respond, Syd said, "Oh, hey!" as if he was only now registering my presence in the house. He quickly closed his laptop. In the weeks to come I would blame this exact moment for rending any connective tissue left between us. Anyone who's torn a ligament would understand the snap of that bond, the sound of foreknowledge, of suffering.

"You got time for a quickie?" At first I wasn't sure he was playing it straight. It had to be a joke. Who asked something like that at a time like this? His face was giving nothing away.

At best, the proximity to flesh was all he needed right now, the only way he knew to fill his emptiness. A stretch, to be sure. My heart turned from him in that moment. I was being shown something about the meaning of my life and our marriage. An answer of sorts, a way to move forward. And although I couldn't know the future, I felt certain I'd be carrying this moment with me a long time into it.

"Um." I waited. "No?"

I shook my head and stormed downstairs, rolled up my sleeves and began clearing the sink, washing the gummy, dried-on ketchup, slamming plates into the dish rack. I knew I was making a clatter. The noise didn't summon Syd from our loft: I continued to hear the music, but no footsteps on the stairs. I wiped my hands dry and stomped to Juliet's room.

I opened her bedroom door and then, gagging, pulled up the blinds and opened the window, leaning out to take a breath. Syd had not entered Juliet's room the whole time I'd been at the hospital—every pot and bowl of vomit was as I'd left it. Seething, I removed each one, holding my breath as I walked them to the toilet, extending my arms in front of me as far as possible. Still holding my breath, I poured the vile yellow liquid down the toilet, inhaling again as I flushed.

Finally I took the pots to the sink and scrubbed them (steely, boiling) with extra soap, piled them next to the other dishes on a towel on the kitchen table; by then the dish rack was completely full.

I turned back to Juliet's room. I found a stack of drawings under her laundry pile: some of our unfinished house, others of my mouth distorted by grimaces. I put them back just as they'd been, fearful of what was to come when Juliet returned. She'd left her bed (a loft bed she'd begged for since about the age of seven and received at eleven or twelve when we found one at a garage sale) unmade.

I climbed the wobbling ladder to the top rung, where Juliet's mattress was ringed by stuffed animals. I curled myself into her body's depression. I cried then, recalling Juliet's words, "I tried to kill myself."

There had to be a piece I wasn't seeing, a mistake somewhere, a misunderstanding. The mind, confounded by questions, froze. The mind was a possum playing dead. I wrapped my arms around Juliet's bedpost, hugging it; the tighter I gripped it, the better I felt. A stick of flotsam in an open ocean. Sun streamed in, my heart slowed. I breathed in, out, in, out.

Finally, I sat up. Wiped my face. I could do this. I would make Juliet's bed. I would make everything comfortable, her room a place where she'd be happy to return. As I was about to take her sheets off, I saw a novel on her pillow; when I picked it up a cardboard note fell out of its pages. It might have been private. But she'd given up that right, so just as I'd opened her journal, I decided to read the note.

The edges of the cardboard were jagged, torn off a box lid. Her writing, like a child's. Large block letters: "I can't live"—the "live" crossed out, followed by "be" instead: "I can't be here anymore." And, on a separate line,

"Goodbye." The final word. The last word that always spoke louder than the rest.

Goodbye?

Goodbye.

How long did I sit on her unmade bed, unmoving, looking down at the torn brown cardboard rectangle, waiting for something to click? Pierce the gut, the heart? For something to make sense. I knew the answer wouldn't leap toward me from the cardboard note, yet I couldn't pull my eyes away. I was still looking when Syd popped his head into the room.

I said nothing about the pots of vomit he'd let fester, about the note I held in my hand. I couldn't. Then, in that way the universe has—trying to give us what we've wanted, just not always in the way we expect, Syd said, "How can I help? I've already hidden the medicine, the keys to the truck, the ropes and cords—"

"What about the guns?"

"She wouldn't shoot herself."

"We don't know *what* she'd do anymore, Syd."

We argued about the guns, and then I agreed to moving the steel gun safe into the trailer, and I ordered Syd to throw all the booze away and I heard the bottles clink in the garbage as he wheeled the can to the street below.

Two days later I found one of the bottles in his toolbox. Three days later he found the mickey I'd rescued while looking for a safety pin in my sewing basket. "We're supposed to be fighting our vices, not each other," I said.

"We're causing damage to Juliet every time we fail."

"You think I don't know that?" he said.

I poured the mickey down the drain.

Driving home, the three of us climbed the long stretch of road, full of potholes and hugging the hill at an angle so steep the truck always seemed as though it might flip backward. Cocooned in its cab, I tried to keep everything casual and upbeat. Juliet said nothing, her lips set into a hardlined grimace. The hospital had reiterated the warning to avoid salt, sour cream, alcohol, drugs, including Tylenol, and sushi, at least for now. Was she thinking about the damage she'd done to herself? I couldn't read her.

In the days to come I would look for liver tonics online. I'd research natural ways to purify and detoxify. Could the damage cause cancer, shorten her life? It broke my heart that she was allergic to the world now. Ron would give me recipes for dandelion tea, the names of naturopaths and numbers for spiritual and physical healers, addresses for alternative medicine clinics in Calcutta and Geneva. I would become an expert on livers.

Now, though, as we climbed upward, I felt a draining away of myself, as if I'd sprung an existential leak.

83

My last vestige of energy sat forgotten on the road below and what was left had collapsed in on itself like a balloon. The closer we got to the house, the worse I felt. Syd, in typical bantering fashion, elbowed me to break the tension and cracked a joke. Juliet kept silently tracing pictures on the window. I lifted my arm to put around her shoulder.

"Take a shower," she said. "You stink."

A middle-aged woman facing a life in tatters. Navvy jack gravel had filled a few potholes but the worst of them lay open, moon craters deep enough to set the truck on three wheels. Meanwhile saplings growing in the ruts scraped the undercarriage clean as we bounced in the cab, hands on the dash to steady ourselves. The engine was on the verge of overheating by the time we made it to the top, the narrow driveway tunnelling through alder trees then suddenly opening into a green, green field, the cabin at its centre, the half-finished house to one side, a dilapidated trailer a short distance away.

Once inside, Juliet went straight to her room. I'd often wondered if her illness was nothing more than her porousness to evil; others had the hard shell of a dung beetle while she moved through the world like a burn victim missing a layer of skin: she seemed to have no immunity, no protection from life's hazards; the poison of the world seeped in. Perhaps Juliet was a canary, a sentinel species, nothing wrong with her except her ability to hear the warning bell of danger.

We sat in the living room. Juliet had gone to sleep. My legs were tucked beneath me, a blanket on my lap. Syd kept his voice low. "Do you think she should go to school tomorrow?" When in doubt, Syd believed in straightforward solutions to complex problems, in simplicity as a virtue. A trait I did not share.

"No," I snapped, "I don't."

Syd looked out the window. Like the wife of Peter, Peter, Pumpkin Eater. In his pumpkin shell, able only to gaze out at the dreary skyline. He ran his fingers through his hair, long now—the motion making his biceps flex. He placed himself squarely in front of the window, looked up half-heartedly toward the ceiling, and shook his head in dismay.

"You can't honestly think she's ready to go back yet," I said.

"I don't know. I know she doesn't need another shrink."

I turned to face him. "She needs as many as it will take."

"Helping is giving her what she needs, not what *you* think she needs. Every time Juliet got in trouble at school, what did you do? Drag her to counselling."

"That's what a parent does."

"That's what *you* do, Rose, bring her to the Altar of Shrinks time and again saying 'Fix her.'"

"I think you're scared of 'shrinks' because of what you might learn about yourself."

"Families don't throw up on a table then invite people to look at the mess. She needs us, not a therapist."

I felt like I was running out of oxygen. Out of breath. "Do you know what she asked me the other day? Whether I thought suicide was a sin."

He shook his head.

"I said I don't think God is cruel, that he would punish a person with a load too heavy to carry."

fourteen

The following week, at the high school, I paced out-side the principal's office, checking my watch again and again. We'd arrived early, Juliet smelling of pot and patchouli and wearing a dress that reminded me of one of my tablecloths, her army surplus boots. From behind the closed door we heard a voice. I didn't know what the result of this meeting would be, but at least Juliet had agreed to it. My hope was that in listening to how other people valued her she'd begin to believe in her own significance.

After a few minutes, the principal stuck his head out. "Juliet. Rose. Come in."

We entered his office and took our seats awkwardly, Juliet with particular effort. Her eyes hidden by sunglasses,

87

YASUKO THANH

she chose a straight-backed chair near the door. The principal asked her to move it closer. Reluctantly, she slid it toward him. I eyed the worn desk, the motley assortment of old and dented filing cabinets, the cheap bookcase, all illuminated by the particular indecency inherent to fluorescent bulbs.

We were joined by her Project Life counsellor who sat juggling a cup of coffee and a breakfast sandwich. I must have looked like a secretary about to take dictation, upright posture, on the edge of my seat, my purse on my lap like a poodle.

The principal, more than six feet tall and built like a rugby player, sat down in a chair meant for a much smaller person and angled himself toward me. "Before we get started. Now that we're all here. Would you like anything to drink? Tea? Coffee? Water?"

Juliet shook her head.

"No, no thank you. I'm good," I said, taking a three-ring notebook out of my purse.

He turned to Juliet. "Your doctor phoned me yesterday and said he really wanted to be here. He emphasized the need for this meeting. He told me your liver has been spared permanent damage. You're very lucky. I'm glad you're here to talk with me."

Juliet shifted and emitted a monosyllabic response. His and the counsellor's attempts to pry into her activities were met by more grunts. I stroked the notebook on my lap then flipped through its pages, looking at no one, disguising my nerves, my surprise at Juliet's behaviour, though the surprise should have been that I'd expected anything different.

She twitched in her seat and pushed up her sunglasses, large and heart-shaped.

Now the principal changed tack. "Have you felt sad again?"

"Nope."

"Would you know if you were?"

"Yup."

"What would you do if that happened?"

She closed her eyes and leaned her head back.

I took a deep breath. "I hope you'd tell me," I said, flexing my mom muscles.

"Would you feel comfortable calling me if that happened?" the principal asked.

I nodded, and he went on to explain why Juliet should return to school, punctuating his speech with an ample amount of throat clearing. He scanned her face intently. Her eyes were still hidden by sunglasses.

Juliet rose suddenly and walked to the door. "I'm not doing this anymore. Mom? Are you coming?"

"Let's all take a break," the counsellor said. "Meet back in fifteen?"

89

I nodded again, grabbed our coats from the backs of our chairs, and chased Juliet down the hall.

I returned to the principal's office, having settled Juliet down in the car. Maybe I should have stayed next to her. Sat in that sadness, a companion, a hand to hold, a shoulder, nothing more or less. Listened. I felt helpless. I knocked twice. The voices stopped. I walked in, feeling like a pupil who'd been sent down for misbehaving, but then such thoughts of unbelonging and imminent punishment had often plagued me.

The principal leaned forward in his chair, loosening his tie. He may have been uncomfortable, nervous, or trying to warn me with this small gesture. He repeated what he'd told me on the phone, that withdrawal wasn't the answer, and added that he was afraid my letting Juliet take the reins would backfire. He seemed to be talking to himself, or perhaps I was too wrapped in self-pity to listen. "We have a program here at the school. It asks students to prioritize their mental health. We call it the Oath of Wellness. It asks them to think about ways they're going to take care of themselves."

I mustered attitude. "I know it from the hospital."

He stiffened, sensing my hostility, moved even further toward the edge of his seat.

I adjusted my skirt. I respected the line polite people do not cross in social situations, yet I had a hard time obeying it when my heart was racing. "I apologize," I said, "for my abruptness. But—"

"It's okay," the principal said. "We know how difficult this is for you."

"The thing we don't want to admit," the counsellor said, "is that, despite our best efforts, the worst that can happen still happens. A cancer patient might still die, even though they're seeing a doctor."

I tried to keep my voice steady. "Knowing you don't want something to happen is different from knowing the steps you need to take in order to stop it."

The counsellor considered me with the intensity of a lip reader, then lowered her eyes. "Some people will kill themselves no matter what intervention takes place."

"There's a . . . a need for control that runs through both of you," the principal noted.

Through Juliet and me? The counsellor and me? I began to speak, then, inevitably it seemed, I broke down. Fumbling now, I opened my purse for a tissue and my notebook slipped to the floor and fell under the chair; as I bent to retrieve it my lighter tumbled out, my compact, loose change.

The principal handed me a box of Kleenex. "We're on your side. We all want what's best for Juliet."

I stared at him. "If someone wants to jump out the window, do you stop them? Most would answer yes, but they neglect to think about the logistics. They don't consider the question, How long do you try? When someone is drowning, threatening to pull you under, how long do you hold on? A day? A week? A year? What does the universe demand?" I knew I was ranting now, but in truth I was terrified.

"You develop the tools. You make a plan."

"What if the plan doesn't work? Or works and then stops? What if the person grows bigger and stronger than you? What then?"

A button on the principal's phone flashed and he looked at his watch.

I took deep breaths. Steadied my voice once more. "Some people might still kill themselves. Not Juliet. She'll never have the chance to try again. I won't let her."

Her counsellor, like her doctor, asked me if I was seeing someone.

fifteen

I exorcized the house with incense bought in bulk from Chinatown wrapped in foil bundles. I scrubbed the hardwood floors and ceilings, the walls, the space heaters, my resentment of Syd continuing to build. He must have felt it; he kept his eyes elsewhere and I kept having to shout, "Look at me when I'm talking to you." Without that I had no way to tell whether what I was saying meant anything, even to myself, my own unworthiness reflected in his averted eyes.

I kept struggling to make myself feel things as real. Where to begin? Who to listen to—the head or the heart? Syd set opposing thoughts and feelings into motion inside me. It had always been this way. At one point early on I'd decided to overlook the fact that Syd, my new lover, was often an asshole. I wasn't surprised when he did things that tore at my heart, and had often thought about leaving him. Just as often, though, fear would whisper in my ear. "You're not smart. You're not pretty. You're not good enough for anyone else."

We both had hard truths to swallow. But swallowing alone wasn't enough; we had to digest those truths, and for that, each of us seemed to be missing an essential part of ourselves. In a way, Juliet had given us a reprieve. With our lives under siege there was no telling how long we could hold the difficult work of ourselves at bay.

Just because we'd believed something in the past didn't mean we had to believe it in the future. Perhaps a day would come when we'd say, scandalized, "Can you believe we once thought death was the end?" Yet Syd held his beliefs so tightly they'd tear before he'd let go. To blame a skewed morality hurt less. I needed to believe he loved me—you see, I too held tight to the fabric of my beliefs.

There was no reason to feel that the universe had turned its back on me, that I'd been cursed. None at all. I had a car, a home, food in the cupboards, yet I'd been set upon by a heavy melancholy. A gilded guillotine that had cut me off from the virtues of faith, hope, and charity.

I developed a fondness for hiding. In the woods behind the house or in the bath with steam and a locked door. I hid from the world. Either something was coming this way and everyone was out to get me or I was so inferior to others in general that I didn't deserve to walk among them. My reflection in the mirror provoked a profound feeling of horror. I couldn't stand myself. And I was afraid.

On a day when, to reinstate normalcy in our lives, Syd and I took a walk along the water, we argued about Juliet.

Her friend Aleeki had come for a visit, and she needed time away from us to be a teenager. "I am entrusting you with her life," I said to Aleeki before we left. "Make sure nothing happens while we're gone."

Syd and I made our way to the seashore under a November sun that gave off little warmth. We strode along at a quick pace, a pace I set, trying to outwalk him, to force him to keep up. In silence we walked. From force of habit, we walked. Still holding hands. Even our strides matched. Yet I barely registered him.

How had we become this?

How did we undo this?

I stopped and photographed houseboats, the passage across the sky of clouds that looked like cauliflower, wind chimes, daffodils. Syd tied a wish he'd written on a piece of paper with a ribbon to a plastic Christmas tree. It was a thing. The notepaper and pencil were attached to its trunk, a silent invitation. Wishes flapped on branches. I didn't know what Syd wrote; I had no idea what he wished; we'd grown that far apart. I watched two young

95

people speaking sign language grow distant at the break-water's end, as if about to step into the waves, and won-dered if they were in love.

We turned in at a tiny restaurant with a sitting area outside. When Syd straddled a plastic chair and drummed the table, I turned away to make him disappear until our fish and chips arrived. Salt, grease, and more salt. I con-sidered the wind's whitecaps of lace. Boats bobbed, and, offshore, cruise ships large as skyscrapers tipped sideways.

We'd not discussed Juliet's continuing absence from school. Syd hadn't brought up the fact that I was still sleep-ing in the hallway outside Juliet's room, as I'd done since her return. Neither had I. We shared silence as a tactic, a sanctuary. I was exhausted from staying awake and check-ing on Juliet at regular intervals throughout the night. At home we shuffled around dazed, snacking on carrots, crackers, sugar peas, pizza crusts, anything crunchy, drag-ging our pain. In all our years together, nothing had pre-pared us for this. Syd wanted to focus on healing, but you had to debride a wound before you stitched the edges back together.

"I called that Assessment and Treatment program," I began, "and made an appointment to see someone about Juliet. Their first opening is six months from now. Can you believe it? Six months that'll make me feel even more pathetic and unable to help her myself."

Syd took my hand and looked at me intently, his eyes seeming darker than usual. "Why'd you do that without asking me?"

"I also phoned a private hospital."

"She'll be surrounded by strangers. You can't rip Juliet from her home the way you tear off a Band-Aid."

"Seriously?" I understood now the meaning of betrayal, the culmination of a battle that had raged between us for years, now more than ever quivering beneath the surface, his hint of a smile, the way he squeezed my arm. On cue, raindrops the size of eggs began to fall.

"Fine. What do you want me to say? It's up to you."

"Don't say it's up to me."

"I want it to be right," he stuttered, "so should—"

"Should I trust your judgment? Should I not trust you? Is that what you're—"

"But you're not trusting me."

"You're telling me. Every time you say it's up to me, it's not."

"It's your call right now."

Our marriage felt like a cloth coming apart in my hands, torn from me bit by bit.

We should have kissed, laid our heads on each other's shoulder, wept, the grey ocean flattening and becoming the horizon, stretching before us. We could have wept at the possibility presented, its openness, a surface waiting to be written upon as though words didn't lie, a blank page, a scroll to cowrite a new script. But in that moment all I felt was a collapse. A shutting down within myself.

Syd began to talk about how his coworkers had rallied around a mistake he'd made at work, telling him, "Dude. You need to see someone."

"What'd they say when you told them?"

They were a good group of guys, rough around the edges. But the kind of guys who understood pain. "I didn't. I haven't."

I was surprised. I knew what big hearts they possessed. I knew his boss and his boss's boss. They'd all have understood a leave of absence to take care of one's own. These men were family men. Now I understood why Syd had so rarely been at the hospital.

He'd been afraid, he said, of their thinking he'd lost his grip on his family. A diminishment of strength.

"What a sorry excuse."

"What about you?"

I'd stopped bothering to eat. Shower. Sleep. Make the bed. I'd be damned if I'd let Juliet take her own life. I would see to it that she never tried again. It was my job to get her the help she needed, which required that she remain alive to receive it. It was what you did with junkies, too. Well, I'd keep her alive until that help came, even if I had to follow her around twenty-four hours a day.

It was known that the average person who tried suicide would reattempt, often in the first month. Founded fears were different from irrational worries. One was specific, one was diffuse. One required action, the other negated it.

I'd seen the truth beyond the veil. That nothing mattered. Except Juliet. Everything, every convention, was part of a road meant to trick me into thinking there was a reason to keep going. It was a road going nowhere. There wasn't a single moment that meant anything in the big picture. That mattered from a cosmic perspective. It would all be dust someday, even Shakespeare. All I knew for sure was that any moment spent away from Juliet was ill spent.

The air was cold enough to see my breath.

I told Syd he wasn't doing his part in holding down the fort. That he always deflected when I asked for help.

"But you always know what to do. As if by *instinct*."

"What a joke. I don't have a clue."

"I don't have it in me," he said.

"I don't either. I'm pulling it out of my ass."

His flattering me in this way, his absolving himself of his inability to nurture, had been his go-to since Juliet was born. I'd missed the silent vote making me primary caregiver. My efforts had culminated in Juliet's suicide attempt. Syd claimed he didn't have it in him, but there was nothing in *me,* either.

I'd caused Juliet's issues, and I was drowning in floodwaters of guilt. I'd never been a good mother. I was worried I was losing the ability even to fake a smile, and terrified at what would happen if it disappeared completely.

I'd failed as a parent. I wasn't too proud to admit that I may have damaged Juliet's brain. There was no way to gauge what my drinking before I'd known I was pregnant had done to her development in utero. I didn't know how to make things right.

"I think you're putting your needs ahead of Juliet's. Living through her. Vicariously. Somehow believing if you stand in the gap between her and the world, then the scared little girl inside you will eventually be healed."

"I never healed. No one ever talked to me."

"You got frozen in time."

He continued talking about all my failures, or that's how I took it, and then a new reality hit me. I was preparing, with my hovering, a lamb for the slaughter. "Fine. I'll just move out. Is that what you want? I can't do this anymore. I can't. I'm just trying to give her what I never had."

"Let her conquer this hurdle. Give her a chance to feel good about herself."

"I'm trying."

"She has to see herself overcoming things."

"When have I not let her do that?"

"You cut her toenails. You flossed her teeth. Over-protective? You were neurotic. You did her homework so she wouldn't get bad grades. And when she got a bad grade, you got all up in her teacher's face."

"Why are you throwing me under the bus?"

"It's practically cheating. And cheaters learn nothing."

"I just wanted to help her."

"Rose. Fuck. That's my point. It's always about *you*. Would it kill you to let go? Just a little bit?"

"Maybe it would. Maybe I'd rather die than let myself become a negligent mother."

"Doesn't that seem a little dramatic? Give her a chance to feel good about herself. Let go."

"Fine. But when she fails and comes to you—let's see if you can stand to see the disappointment in her face. See herself beating herself up over it. Let's see you deal with it. You were the one who couldn't care less about the grades she got in high school. It's not like I did all her homework."

"Just take a breath."

We headed back to the house. "Hey, I didn't mean for this walk to go sideways," Syd blurted. "It's just—" He paused. "I want to die, too," he said. "Sometimes."

Shock overwhelmed me. "How long have you been feeling this way?"

"Years," he said.

We returned home to find Juliet scribbling "End Me" on the birch tree with sidewalk chalk.

Syd paced the house. Lately, he'd been doing a lot of pacing. Meanwhile, I cleaned. Since Juliet's return I'd washed clothes, fuckit, washed dishes, fuckit, made the beds. Fuckit. Took out the garbage, fuckit, which had started to smell because I'd waited too long. Fuckit. Juliet sensed the distance between Syd and me.

Each day proved more difficult than the last. I feared trivial words that led to responses I didn't want and couldn't manage. I held my head in my hands, pressed my fingers into my brows so hard my eyes watered. My brain, zapping. Was it my lobes or was it life malfunctioning? Fuckit, fuckit, fuckit. What was the payoff? Who knew? But the fuckit, like an old friend, remained.

After breakfast, Juliet would watch *Tales of Mystery and Imagination* in bed and eat popcorn: I knew from experience that children were experts in hiding their feelings and that her moderately happy exterior was, in and of itself, not a reason not to worry. She dug deeper under her blankets, as black as her sheets and curtains. On the screen a sculptor hacked off his model's limbs.

"May I join you?" I felt trapped, the same way I had when Juliet was a baby. Then I noticed black widow egg sacks hanging from the cupboard beneath her TV. I swept the spiders into an empty jam jar, and then, fuelled by the neurotic conviction that I'd prove my love for Juliet, put my hand inside with an uneasy jolt of liftoff, telling myself that none of these spiders were going to bite me. I was a good mother. I loved Juliet.

sixteen

I left Juliet and Åleeki on the porch sharing YouTube videos. She was safe, for now, but I was anxious to leave her. I took the trail to Ron's through the goldenrods in blue mid-morning light and saw a commotion from the corner of my eye. Black movement of wings, featherless heads bent around a body in the grass, five birds circling. The crows, hopping foot to foot on the sidelines, withdrew reluctantly. I approached. The turkey vultures were the size of coyotes and a little scary; they too retreated, tucking themselves into the trees. A dead doe. Her soft coat compelled me and I reached out to place my warm palm against her, pausing to acknowledge this delicate dance of deer and poplar linking the green grass to the bright sky.

After pushing Ron's gate open by its deer-antler handle I passed under the driftwood archway, nearly hitting my head on a hanging fishing ball. I stepped over a hose on the grass and ran the gauntlet of Tibetan prayer flags that hung between large cedars. Strange statues, deities, lived in the forest beyond the smokehouse and the chicken coop, in plain sight from Ron's porch; they peeked out from plants in his garden that had since grown around them, the mystical and the vulgar, posed insanely in lovemaking positions that contorted their bodies in ways I would not have thought physically possible. Of course, they were gods, and gods could do anything with their bodies, even defy the Reaper.

A rusting "Ignition' Services" sign leaned against the wall of Ron's house. A robin tugged a worm from the black, toxic-looking puddle, attempted to clean it on the grass, wiping it back and forth, without terrible success. In the end it hopped away with the worm in his beak.

I found Ron out by the split-rail fence, working on his Jeep, half a pack of cigarettes open on the hood, motor oil puddling in a patch of clover.

"I'm going crazy," I said by way of hello.

"You want to see something really crazy?" Ron said he'd bought two new corn snakes the day before. We walked to the garage; forty venomous snakes in tanks slithered under heat lamps. I plugged my nose against the stench. My adrenalin rose. Ron denied there was any risk and told me I worried too much. I think he just liked the feeling of danger in his hands, liked manipulating it, trying to tame it.

"You still starting up that natural vibration farm?"

"Yes."

"I think I'm getting sick. Not sick and tired, but actually sick."

Ron, who fancied himself an expert in traditional Chinese medicine, told me to describe the pain. Afterward he said my discomfort was a physical manifestation of oppression, the word itself from the Latin, "pressed against," as in against a rock and a hard place.

"I thought it was heartburn," I said.

"Think about it. What's heartburn? A burning heart, a heart on fire, just another day of what Chinese practitioners call Phlegm Heat in the Heart, oppression flattening out the soul." Ron leaned down, his shell necklaces tapping, and removed one of the snakes, making a soft clacking sound. "When I start the natural vibration farm, you're the first person I'll cure."

"You know, I flipped a coin about whether I should come here today." I told Ron that when in doubt about any course of action, any venture large or small, I'd flip a coin and let luck decide. Yes or no. Life or death. Hello. Goodbye. This had always been successful.

He put the snake back in its tank and rested his hand on top of mine.

"And? Are you glad?"

"I'm not sure. I'm trying something new, but it's scary."

"Coffee?"

We moved into the living room. As he fetched the coffee I surveyed the walls, which showcased musical instruments from around the world as well as sand he'd saved in bottles from every place he'd been. All my life I'd wanted to be a travel photographer: maybe Ron could show me how. He put a mug in my hand and sat next to me on the couch. Behind us the floor-to-ceiling windows let light fall in through the open curtains. A seagull flew past.

He spoke to me in an intimate way he never had before, told me about his brother, a gay minister, who hadn't come out of the closet until he'd contracted HIV. He told Ron only after he'd been admitted to the hospital for the last time, swearing Ron to secrecy. This was back in the days before AZT.

Ron had watched his brother get sicker. "He was a total artist. A total intellectual. You would have loved him."

"What a great burden. I mean for him, of course, but for you too. To have to carry that secret."

"It was. But I had to respect his wish. In the end, he was so bitter. He lashed out."

"At the disease?"

"At himself. For being gay. Because that's what had put him there. He thought if he'd never lived the lifestyle . . . that was the only way he knew how to repent. To call himself a faggot."

"It's not as if he had a choice."

"But at the end he thought he had—his self-hatred was so bad he thought he'd done it to himself. You know what the funny thing is? It brought our family together. He was so afraid, but in his last days, when I could tell the family, there was no judgment. Father, mother, brothers, sister, we all rallied around him. He died surrounded by love."

Ron's candour broke me open, and a torrent of words (whose flow could be directed but not stopped) spilled out of the crack. In the cheeriest voice I could manage (and why was it important that it be cheery?), I talked to him about Juliet. "Imagine a tornado, and that you're holding on for dear life. Flowerpots, bicycles, the roofs of houses, they're all flying into the sky. I think for her it was like the world was being sucked up around her, pieces of it vanishing into air, everything she knew breaking into bits. That's what I think happened to Juliet. She was holding on. But her arms got tired."

"That's a good point. No one blames someone for getting sucked into a tornado."

"Right?"

"But they blame suicides."

Both of us had tears in our eyes.

"Yeah." I laughed, a loud, jagged sound.

"Is she at least happy to be home?"

"I'm on death watch."

"Geez."

"Thing is, no matter what she'll always be a flight risk. She'll always be a person who wanted to die, and even if the years to come are okay, nothing can change the fact of what happened. If something is staked on hope, it's called a gamble. I don't want her life to be a gamble."

I told Ron about the state in which I'd found Juliet's room in the vein of a Can You Believe It? story. But Ron didn't respond with righteous shock. "Men are such pigs," he said.

"Syd thinks I'm preparing, with my hovering, a lamb for the slaughter. He thinks I'm living *through* her to heal the little girl in me. Could he be right?"

"I don't think so."

"You don't think I'm trying to protect her, because of my own pain?"

"I don't think it matters why. Just that you do."

"Me too. I mean, I see it as my duty, my mission, to stand between Juliet and pain. Shield her from hurt. I would do anything for her."

"Everything your mother didn't do for you . . ."

"Exactly. It's my calling. My sole mission on earth."

"You're a lovely woman."

"Syd would call it pathological. Do you know I caught him reading about Munchausen Syndrome by Proxy?"

"Isn't that where parents make their kids sick?"

I nodded.

"The last thing you need is blame." Ron was never shocked. I could say anything I wanted, knowing he wouldn't run away. I offloaded, took advice, ranted. He'd come over in the morning for a coffee. Coffee stretched into the afternoon. I'd fix us lunch, or not. Lunch stretched into tea; we'd still be sitting at the kitchen table when Syd got home from work. In the beginning, Syd seemed pleased that Ron listened to my troubles; it lessened his load. I liked the way Ron held his place. I liked that whether Syd was home or not Ron acted like a mountain that would not be moved. Not obnoxiously. In the beginning, when Syd came home and Ron was over, I'd rise quickly from the table, inviting Ron to stay for dinner, start prepping our meal. I'd fix everyone dinner and gave Juliet her plate so that she could eat in her bedroom the way she wanted. Later, though, I didn't get up right away. Later, when Syd came in and saw Ron, he'd go straight to the loft.

These days Syd and I would argue about whether Juliet should sit at the dinner table. She *wanted* to eat in her room, I'd say. She wanted to stay up for days playing video games. Fine. She wanted to sleep for days, fine. I didn't push her to go back to school. I wasn't pushing her to do anything: I felt that my task was to help her understand the nature of her own want. How to recognize her own needs and how to respect them. In other words, how to listen to herself. How to create the kind of life that was right for her. How to live in the kind of world she could see herself in. It was my role to help her build a radical acceptance of herself. I thought the best way to do this was by letting her do whatever she wanted.

And yet still I didn't sleep. Tired as I was, I couldn't allow myself to succumb; it would feel like a betrayal. From our bedroom a floor above I'd be too far away to prevent Juliet from harming herself. How could I allow myself that luxury? Falling asleep terrified me for another reason. I'd lie there in the quiet and the worries would begin. The loop of circular thoughts. I turned over Juliet's explanation for why a thousand times. Too happy. I tried to define happiness. Was it even real? I understood perverted desires. But happiness? How did one pin down that slippery notion?

Nights, I devised ways to keep myself awake. I forced myself to read. I'd buy whatever books I thought might help: *Final Gifts: Understanding the Special Awareness, Needs, and Communications of the Dying; Dying and Death; Death as a Fact of Life; Last Rites; How We Die; Into This Wild Darkness.* I'd drag my blanket, cape-like, to retrieve one from the shelf and station myself in the hallway, on the wood floor, right outside Juliet's bedroom, always fearing another attempt. I'd put the duvet ripped beyond sewing, fabric too thin to hold stitches (though I'd tried four times before resorting to duct tape) in front of her door, my toes catching on the holes. One night I stayed awake rereading Alice Munro's *Too Much Happiness.* I remade my bed. Tried to get comfortable, staring at the door crack, lying stiffly on my side, cold under my blanket, wondering where the draft was coming from. I made mental lists. I watched *Cold Case Files* and *Trauma: Life in the ER,* not to see crimes solved or heroics in action but for the death. Gathering information. I had no choice. Everything hung in the balance of my discovering why Juliet had wanted to die. Not knowing was not an option. In other words, to be a good mother I had to know. If I couldn't discover why, I might as well have snapped that little baby's neck myself as soon as I saw her scrunched-up boxer's face in the delivery room.

Now, with the internet as my answer key, I mingled as if at a cocktail party, learning my enemy's habits and traits, becoming aware of her various disguises. By meeting Death's friends and acquaintances, by learning all their names, their tendencies, I'd be better equipped to stop her. Whereas before I'd gone to YouTube for how to roast a chicken, how to build a table, how to choose a guinea pig, now I learned about Death. The cold beauty of a surgeon's scalpel exploring the innermost parts of a human being. The myriad ways a body ceased to function. The precision with which opponents inflicted injury on each other, examples of the ability to endure pain and keep going, what it meant to keep getting beaten down and pop back up and do it all without flinching. The lack of feeling serial killers exhibited in their work, or doctors on the front line who couldn't afford to care about each person coming into the trauma bay. I watched bare-knuckle boxing. I thought of Jesus, the martyr. The God in us all who measured love by how much had been sacrificed and talked a lot about "heart" just as mixed martial arts fighters did before a match.

Juliet's life depended on my looking for the answers I found. I searched online as if I had no choice, as if what I needed would be found on the hundredth site. The role

113

of advocate was too small for me. The role of hawk was better, but I saw it wearing on Juliet.

I called it caring. She called it lack of trust. Still, every hour, with the need of an addict, I'd poke my head into her room to make sure she was breathing. I tried to stop myself, but couldn't, as if I could enfold her under my wing and keep her there. I'd stand at her door and listen to her shift in bed, roll over. Her nails pink as seashells, her mouth open in a sigh; seen from the right angle she appeared to be smiling, just as she used to do even when she thought no one was watching, glowing from the inside, amused at a private joke between her and the universe—her breaths were shallow, not the deep snores of REM sleep. When she slept: Did she hear voices? What did she dream?

What if Syd was right? What if my overprotectiveness was more about me than Juliet? Maybe I'd become addicted to protecting her, to the reassurance it provided me. What if I was addressing my own childhood pain rather than Juliet's risk levels? What if I'd been deluded all along—not a good mother anchored to life but an injured animal dragging my traumas and open wounds behind me?

All I knew for sure is that if I stayed awake life would continue. The world would not quit me. If I continued being vigilant, the world would exist. To stop, to

114

let go, would be fatal, an astronaut in space letting go of the thread that had held him to the ship in that cold, black weightlessness. We'd all seen that movie. Come on. The last, heartbreaking scene with a white spacesuit against the tar-coloured void floating away, growing ever smaller, drifting out of sight and into the nothingness that surrounded us all. If we stopped. If anyone stopped. Whatever their version of staying awake was.

I slept only when Juliet did, tried to wake up before her. Her sleep patterns were as erratic as a moth's flight. She'd stay up until three a.m., or six a.m., would lose the day to sleep or would awake after two hours. Naps performed as the role of understudy to healing, but poorly, leaving her brain and bones exposed to the cacophony of an unruly crowd. They booed and jeered. They yelled, "Why don't you give it up already? Why don't you give up?" I was her mother. I'd brought her into this world and would be damned for sticking around to guide her out of it. That was not how it was supposed to happen. I wouldn't let it.

I typed "suicide" and "method" and "statistical success" into Google's search engine. Until I educated myself, I'd be punching in the dark. Taking hits from every direction. I learned that goldfish died in bowls when their organs outgrew their body. The lesson was clear: those who lived in a world too small for them would eventually explode.

I searched for photos online: A dead baby girl lay in the arms of her mother. A baby in a pram. A small boy on a daybed. I studied their closed eyes, lured by their faces. I'd never have another child. The truth of a photograph was in its ability to astonish: each was a catastrophe, an intractable reality. A postcard from the 1920s showed a young girl in cotton stockings, her coffin propped against a wall, the bed cover, a makeshift backdrop. A pencilled inscription at the bottom of the frame read, "*There's a silver lining in the clouds for me.*" The final meaning of a photograph was simple: "That has been."

Our honeymoon photo on the mantel. That has been. Two faces on white hotel pillows. In the moment it had felt right. Perfect. True romantics who, once having found each other, needed only each other. Nothing else on earth. Bonnie and Clyde against the world. In the photo you could see the neck of a yellow dress I was wearing and the pearl snaps on Syd's shirt. *Wedding Night!*—that's what the photo said on the upper-right corner in ballpoint pen. But it wasn't the inscription I noticed first. Nor Syd's half-closed eyes, the shot taken mid-blink. I was captivated by all the air. The air between our fingers, between our bodies. We were together but apart, and what lay between us formed all the space in which we were not. The call of the void, impossible to hear it and look away.

A few weeks after our wedding Syd had asked me,

"So, you're not going to change now, are you? Suddenly become a different person?"

"The me you see is the real me."

The answer satisfied him. But I'd made a mistake. Life throws punches and you have two choices. Only an idiot doesn't change their stance, stands there, unmoving, a target. I *had* changed, I conceded. Had I had a choice? Syd hadn't prepared for life to throw things at him, but neither had I. Still, you had to try. I'd first gotten together with Syd believing he'd reward my devotion with a deep recognition of my worth, raising my flatlined self-esteem in the process. How naive. How childish. How whacked to have ever thought such reciprocity was even to be desired. People don't "complete" each other. Nobody could be bothered.

I felt homesick without knowing where home was. I couldn't control the things that mattered most. I must have slept because I dreamed. I was in danger and Syd out of reach. Strangely, Juliet did not appear in these dreams. The capacity children had to love even the worst parent was second to none: my wishes clung to that thread.

One night Syd saw me on the floor. It was nearly midnight.

"I'm taking you to the doctor tomorrow," he said. "Can you please be open-minded if the suggestion of psych meds comes up?"

The next day I was given a prescription for escitalo-
pram along with a box of ulcer medication and told to
drink Metamucil three times a day. What the doctor
couldn't possibly have known at the time (I didn't either,
at the time) was that I needed Syd. Not meds. And I was
fascinated by my own fear of how much I needed him,
and the horror it invoked. I continued to try to believe
the lies I had told myself about my ability to protect her,
but Aleeki's call late one night pointed to the contrary,
and corroborated Syd's point of view.

seventeen

The dying one sits up, talks about train tickets, or needing to find their passport, wanting to go home, reaching for a figure only their glazed eyes can discern. Is the process of dying the same for those who linger with, say, cancer, a dimming of the light, as it is for those whose death takes place in a flash? As Juliet was ridding herself one by one of her paintings, did she go through the stages of denial, anger, bargaining, and acceptance? Was she visited by her grandmother? Or an angel? Young people, wounded, before succumbing to their injuries, hid it. They held their own, chatting right up to the very minute they died. I think about part of Juliet dying as she made dinner. As she watched a movie. Juliet said the universe paid you back for the things you'd lost.

I'd lost three men in two years, then Syd bought me an orange. Marriage is a gamble. Like blackjack. You have to play without seeing into the future, not knowing the dealer's hand. Yet you move forward. You up the stakes. There's no other way to play, if you want to. It comes down to that: you either play or you don't.

But it couldn't have been a love of blackjack alone. What need in me did the belief that true love existed— that it needed to be captured, without hesitation, like a bird on a branch—what need did it fill? One might say the need came simply from wanting love, like any other human being. Or a deep conviction that love was everything.

Before Syd, my life had been in the hands of strange men in the backseat of cars; my life had been the drive home, wondering who was sharing my skin like a glove, always putting her tits where they didn't belong. I'd considered a tattoo on my ass that said "Enjoy the ride." I wanted hands to shape me, to stop me, to tell me I was crazy. I begged and yet remained lost, looking for fingers to touch me as I floated down highways like fog. Deep down I thought I was bent, bad, and broken—and I was too petulant to look deep down inside myself to discover otherwise. Working at the bar where I'd met Syd, I'd loved rebels of every kind, poets, good old boys with 4x4s, musicians, addicts. I was wild for sin and whisky, wild for wilderness over the ceases and desists, the sober facts. Hunger for love sharpened my mind. Drinking caused blackouts. Flashes of memory yelling "Surprise" in a room where all the lights had been turned off. A single scenic burst: A sidewalk rising to meet me. My purse open in my lap on a bus. Dumpsters in a parking lot, waking in my bed with a blinding headache and no recollection of how I got there, pitying myself, claiming the human right to be melancholy. I drank to feel alive but maybe I only felt alive when I was killing myself.

And all because my mother died. I drank to numb. I drank to escape.

After my mother died, my father checked out and I had no choice but to take on adult responsibilities far too quickly. I learned to cook dinners, do laundry. I saw my classmates go to parties, get drunk, fall in love, while I held down the fort, wanting to be like them, wanting that freedom. I sucked in my sadness and my father praised my bravery. He wasn't unkind, just unseeing. I wanted to live, or what I thought was living, then, but instead I had to look after my father, and take my mother's place at the table. By the time my father remarried, the die had been cast. I had formed no true friendships. Not because I hadn't been lonely, but because my studies had left no time for friendships. I threw myself into my schoolwork. I saw my education as my ticket out.

Walking home one day, I saw a Help Wanted sign.
I became a dishwasher around the corner from a strip club.
When I found out how much money the dancers made,
even though it went against every moral fibre of my being,
I began stripping.

Each of us is born with certain abilities: mine is leaping
before I look.

The strip club where I danced was close to Chinatown,
with the cheapest pints in the city and an international
hostel upstairs. It was decorated to look like a brothel with
red cushions and red floors. Every customer came from
away and had a personal melodrama to share. The artists
and intellectuals who gathered there, in that club, were
angry at a capitalist society. Their drunken discussions sat-
urated the room. I normally disparaged idealists as well
as that breed of self-proclaimed pilgrim who carried his
soul on the outside like a suitcase, who refused to examine
his dirty laundry on a table but instead looked for his self
in a bar, as if he could happen to stumble upon it. Back
then I lived with malaise like a hermit on a mountain, a
dog as sole source of company. The tedium of my job
did not reflect the excellent quality of the management
of the club; rather, it resulted from the number of years
I'd been a ruthless dancer. Even my ruthlessness bored
me. In my race for money I'd lost my joy. In seeing the
worst of people I'd lost my humanity. In other words, my

122

drinking and pre-existing tendencies toward melancholy had culminated in a pathology that left me increasingly sulky. I waited, with no degree of certainty, for The One (much like Juliet) to release me from my holding pen.

The night I met Syd, I asked him about his love life. He cultivated an air of mystery that I mistook for good breeding. I thought I had him pegged and invented him a story: a woman had jilted him, a woman who'd failed to understand the way passion verges on possession, taints the heart when misunderstood. Putting myself in his place, I could then imagine how Chinatown beckoned, and I set him apart from those pilgrims who'd stuffed their backpacks with guidebooks, underwear, and questions about their role in the world. Under the covers with Syd I shrank, and liked it. I liked the mindlessness of sex, how the moment (small as the head of a pin) revealed itself to me (I danced on it effortlessly). It was intense. And easy, quick.

That might have been my first warning. I should have questioned our leap into a love affair that fast. In hindsight, it was a red flag. Normal people didn't drop everything in life to be with each other.

Here was the truth: people dropped out of life only when they didn't have one. We should have questioned our sprint toward commitment as we raced there in the first heady days and weeks.

123

Though I danced for a living, I was essentially a prude.
I wanted to climb out of my shell to try the art of *shibari*.
I saw it was beautiful. Intricate patterns of delicately tied
rope, known as *asanawa*, competed for attention with the
flesh; the rope itself, hemp and jute, in bondage art, com-
municated meaning: an extension of hands, his arm. His
arm. Covered in nautical tattoos. The anchors fell away
first, then the pig, the cock. Edgy, symbolic power. I took
to my new miniature world, and like Gulliver infecting the
world of the Lilliputians there was no going back. That's
why he stayed, why I let him stay. We conjoined through
bondage, addressing old hurts with new pain, an exercise involving both restraint and freedom, a euphony of
opposites; he said he saw his own best self reflected in my
veil of sweat, his best thoughts, his best values, and I was
startled to see who I was in the mirror surface of another
human being. The cool sheet under our thighs cemented
it. No going back. To write a love poem was not to get to
the heart of it, and less than we deserved. I smelled those
reductions, clichés, prowling far from home. I hated how
any poem's sense curled up like a cat, how every story was
about the same thing, falling in love, or payback, or going
places you didn't want to go. But was it?

Syd was on parole. Small signs gave away his jailhouse
past—he ate his complimentary meal from the club with
his forearms on the wooden bar, leaning over his burger,

guarding the plate. Most clubs had turned him away, but the owner was an ex-con and Syd no stranger to taking punches and bottles and knives and, one time, a gun, and Syd, who would have let everyone in and whose motto was live and let live, needed the money and money was money. When I learned he'd done time the irony delighted me, that he, a man rejected by the world, was now choosing whom to reject in one small part of it, a gatekeeper for a nightclub where bohemianism was a function of the lighting and music and joss sticks were always burning.

I had a view toward a Beaver Cleaver life. I craved its (fictional) simplicity, its wholesomeness; Syd, more than ten years older than I, favoured ethics-made-easy; neither of us knew the steps to take to get to the picket-fenced yard and summers full of sunshine and a backyard swing. All we had was craving. We clutched our desire and the hidden expectation that the other would deliver what we'd dreamed.

We were two bumbling kids trying to find our better natures, prevented by something within us from ever getting it right. We'd try and try but the light always eluded us, always seemed just over the next hill, a sunrise we followed. That I follow still.

After we'd moved in together, we began noticing things about the other we didn't like; by then it was too late. That he'd spent twelve years in prison, having gone in at sixteen and come out at twenty-eight, having never done the usual things like getting an apartment, signing a lease, making a budget, learning how to cook. That his journey inside himself to search for the teenage boy he'd been and had lost was blocked every night by a dead man's face, by the night terrors from which he awoke screaming.

Syd had been sentenced for accidentally killing his uncle while stepping in to protect his aunt from his uncle's domestic abuse. I didn't press, because a thing pressed will close in on itself, while something given space will emerge in its own time. He understood, now, that the word for it was shock. At the time he thought: I must have to be a psychopath.

On his release he moved across the country to put as much distance between himself and his family's dysfunction. Syd feared he could kill again—feared the part of himself that felt nothing when his uncle fell to the ground and stayed there, unmoving. He dreamed of going to Thailand, of losing himself. He didn't have the money, ex-con, no good work, but he saved what he could. Thailand. Cuba. A month. A year. He'd know, feel the shedding, the sliding off, when he'd lost what he came to lose. Free, naked, resting under every green tree.

I once asked him, "How do you think your old self will feel about being left behind?"

Because I asked it of myself.

Outside our window the bar sign, flicking red into the room, rotated, its glow softened by a curtain of vines that hung from the power lines, obscuring our view of the narrow alley below. Most days, that seemed enough. Then, when I discovered I was pregnant, we turned into an experiment neither of us felt willing to abandon. Syd claimed to want a child so much that his travel plans went out the window and he put his offer on the table. "Just give birth. Give birth and I'll do everything," he'd said.

We married the following summer, right before Juliet was born, as if testing the gods to see whether lightning would strike the church, electrifying the jive band in its annex, or whether a flood on our three-day honeymoon 127 would wash out the road from Florence to Newport or sweep us downriver, sinking us into the deep blue water of the lake between the mountains. After we got home (our bond uncontested by supernatural powers, the gods having spoken) Syd worked at the shipyard unloading containers— clothes, grain, luxury cars, stereos—from ships, exotic names on their hulls. To the west of the ports, the arm of the river, orange cranes resembling giant ostriches moving in synchronicity; to the east, train tracks, birds picking at wheat fallen from boxcars between railway ties. I remembered mornings when looking at Syd asleep in bed made me feel as though I'd unwrapped a gift on my birthday.

Gazing into that long mirror of what had been, I understood that my best days had passed me by. Juliet's childhood would never come again, yet I'd let the time slip away like blemished coins through my fingers. What had I been thinking? I'd been entrusted with a gift that should have gone to a woman with knowledge of precious things. Such a beautiful child. Blue eyes that turned green as she got older. Black eyelashes. Blond hair. A beautiful child. Everyone said so. Juliet slept next to me every day through her infancy, having been born thirsty. She breastfed around the clock. Her endless thirst drove me to hate my own breasts, their capacity to make milk, and by the time she was six months old I was at the end of my rope. In exhaustion I paced with her in my arms, muttering, "What's wrong with you?"

Syd said she was the best thing that had ever happened to us and then left most of the child rearing, the day-to-day discipline, the school lunches, the parent–teacher meetings, the birthday parties to me. He loved her the way he loved ambient music. We stayed together yet journeyed apart, each inside ourselves, beyond time, beyond space; we closed in, blinded by the commonplace condition of a need to be elsewhere, to run, from a depression inescapable because it was within.

128

Juliet with skinned knees and a BMX bike, pigtails, the braces she wore for the same overbite I used to have. Juliet, jumping all over the bed in slippers and pyjamas, yelling, "I'm a mean mean fighting machine." Juliet, combing tidal pools, turning stones to find crabs, stuffing herself with blackberries bursting from their skins. I worked in the garden; she squatted beside me and pulled out weeds. When we grocery shopped, she carried the basket and put the ketchup, macaroni, and yogurt on the conveyor belt. She smiled, showed off her missing front teeth, flattening her tongue against the gap "in the shape of a heart," she announced proudly. Juliet was the type of child who grew energetic when tired, pulled books from shelves, chased the cat, bit me and said she was a vampire. Syd said I sweated the small stuff.

He was mistaken. If anything, I wasn't involved enough. Juliet had found the space to attempt suicide, begging off early, going to her room, closing the door.

We'd been trying to straighten ourselves out since the day she was born. But Juliet. Juliet was smart. Smarter than either one of us. She could spell her own name and paint her own toenails at three; at four she observed that if one unrolled a French horn it would be longer than our living room; at five she informed me that a mother squid would rather eat her own tentacles than deprive her offspring of food. Syd and Juliet shared an important look, then, as if I'd missed a joke, and as her intellect grew, the more they colluded over me, sometimes in good humour. I let go. If it were to cause her to grow up and be nothing like me, so much the better. You could punish her but it did no good. She showed no emotion whatsoever over four weeks of rescinded desserts, and it was Syd who'd made her tough. Syd, with the attitude of a farmer figuring if it was on its feet it's okay, who rough-housed with her, taught her how to bind the wing of a broken bird to its body, where to strike a stone on an animal too injured to survive, who taught her mercy. I taught her drama. According to Syd.

When she was seven I found her standing on the roof outside her bedroom window. Rain-wet shingles, a steep pitch.

I told her to climb back inside.

"Why?"

"Because I said so."

"No."

"What are you doing?"

"Looking."

"At least sit down."

"I don't want to."

I coaxed her back from the eave, concentrated on keeping the panic from my voice. Grass below. To soften the blow. Enough? She wouldn't die. Might break a bone.

Unless she swan-dived. Finally, Juliet complied. That afternoon, I called our doctor.

"You're being melodramatic," Syd said.

Looking after a suicidal child is keeping watch, tuning into vibrations like a spider in a web, feeling for incursions, the rain before the storm that sends a tree crashing into the house, the sound of glass breaking, making meals and never knowing if she'll be alive to eat them. The legal details of death alone would be unimaginable; how did anyone cope with arrangements in sorrow? Being terrified of sleep, my God, who could sleep; I didn't understand how Syd could, how he could do anything, how he could go through the motions, the motions of living, trusting the forward passage of time. I was trapped in an hourglass, sand covering my head.

Over the years Juliet became a teenager, asked for homework help; dishes dirtied the sink, the porch light died, yet neither Syd nor I was present; we came to the dinner table half-there, one version of ourselves sitting in front of a placemat, tapping our feet. Juliet saw other doctors. She had difficulty in relating to people. She misread subtle social signals. The medical profession concluded that she was fine. I was an alarmist. Syd thought so.

I'd been vindicated in the worst way.

Still, as far as our friends knew, I was a good mother and Syd and I were a solid couple; we'd never been visited by Social Services. Syd and I mostly drank at home, together, in front of the television, instead of taking turns going to the bar. To be fair, Syd went to work every day, giving us the means to be us, a family, happy from the outside. My income was gravy. I spent almost all of it on books for Juliet. The perfect family from the outside, visiting the museum every Saturday, culture an expense I never scrimped on.

Juliet swam in the bay with a toy keyboard sealed in a freezer bag so that she could play music for the fish. I wondered what song. I never asked her.

I brought it up years later. Juliet said she had no clue what I was talking about.

"I've never, ever had a Fisher-Price keyboard," she said.

132

eighteen

Juliet grew more resentful of my hovering, a look of
disgust clotting behind her eyes the way the storm clouds
did outside the window. "Whatchyou got planned for
today?" I asked. Juliet lay splayed-limbed on the couch
watching TV. "Dunno." She lifted her head; I passed by on
my way out the back door, a trowel in my hand.

"You going to look for work?"

She said, "I'd rather kill myself." And laughed.

I wanted to laugh too, to pretend she was joking, to
live like the gods for whom nothing was sacred. "Okay,"
I said. "Well, put our number in a plastic bag so that if
you're found we can be told." But my joke landed with
a thud.

Horrified at myself, I escaped into the backyard.

The massive evergreens that flanked the yard had covered the trampoline in pine needles that clung to spiderwebs and caught in my clothes; I began sweeping its vinyl covering. Alligator lizards skittered, grey-green flashes; on the springs, two missing tails.

Juliet had broken her arm on this trampoline. I'd been grocery shopping and had pulled into the drive to see Syd double-bouncing her higher than the fruit trees; my stomach turning, I hurried past them up the walkway clutching the paper bags to my body and saying, "You're scaring me."

Not long after, Juliet came into the house, whimpering a little, not crying. Said she'd fallen, her arm hurt. I asked her to wiggle her fingers, to bend her elbow, her wrist. That evening I dragged her to Ron's party, not knowing. Juliet fell asleep on the couch; guests mingled, balancing plates of hors d'oeuvres and shouting at each other two feet from her over the band.

Strange, I thought, that she can sleep with all this noise. I sang "Barrett's Privateers" along with Ron because it was Canada Day. I waited two days before taking Juliet for X-rays. "Growing up is what they do," Ron said to me once, raising his whisky glass, "with or without us." The thing is, when you have a break like that, little bits of bone go floating around in your blood. Her arm had snapped in three places. An ordeal of pins and surgery followed, then months of physical therapy. Every time Ron asked how she was doing, I told the story of how tough she was and how rotten I was, turning his backyard into a confession booth. "Her ability, it horrified me to learn," I told him, "was to swallow her own pain."

Juliet loved that trampoline, running into the back-yard in the rain to squirt it with dish soap before bouncing, loving the bubbles, loving the rain, the chestnut tree's huge leaves like umbrellas; she'd pull the corner of a leaf, showering herself. Later I'd hold the front screen door open with my leg, yell, "Juliet! Come inside! Aren't you freezing?" But in the rain, arms outstretched, the porch light illuminating her, she'd close her eyes and turn her face skyward, catching drops on her tongue. I envied her and her enclosure within the world she'd created. She was enclosing, protecting, her freedom, as if within her domain there was nothing *but* freedom, flowing with the vitality of pure mountain air.

nineteen

The morning after that long-ago party I woke up in pain, flipping a coin to decide whether I'd get up or stay in bed. My head hurt, a chamber I couldn't escape covered in broken glass. The sky pressed down. Closet, bed, armoire, pencil skirt, my breath tight and clenching. The light, constant and contrary. Caged muscles straining toward the furthest point. Our house overloaded with books and things and people. No room to stretch here. Our lives were a story, and I wanted to have the chance to write my own ending.

I went for a walk. I wore stockings and my favourite pumps, black with tiny leather bows. I wore a vintage suit with a Peter Pan collar. A car accelerated behind me and beyond the bridge cicadas droned, birds twittered, a rooster crowed. Flies in sunlight hovered over long grass by the roadside. An inexplicable sense of dread, the sense of an ending, imbued the high clouds, the bright green skirts of cedar trees, the so soft wings of seagulls. The heat added to this feeling.

I paced nonstop from one end of the trestle bridge to the other for a full half hour. Syd's comment the night before had cleaved me: he'd pointed at my ponytail and sweatpants, and said, "That," then, pointing at his crotch, "isn't working for *this*."

I'd been wearing the same dirty clothes for days on end, gathering my greasy hair into an elastic and putting on a baseball cap. Or I'd wear a bathrobe over my ski jacket and pyjamas, which, these days, I didn't bother to change out of in the morning. They were the warmest pyjamas I owned, fleece. No reason to dress in the morning; you were only going to undress again at night.

I'd thought our sex life was adequate. I hadn't realized that it hinged on my looks, or my clothes.

I'd stared at my face in the mirror a long time. I'd touched my crow's feet, examined the marionette lines drawing my mouth toward my chin, unable to shake the feeling that I'd failed, even in a place where, to the competition, dressing up meant matching your gumboots to your baseball cap.

My waist against the guardrail, I balanced over the water, arms and feet hanging over a carpet of green. From the first slab of stone spanning rapids, from the first tree to fall across a ravine, a bridge over obstacles was a monument to great ambition, defiant in the face of gravity's pull. An animal, I'd once read, used to be pushed onto the bridge first, a pig or a dog sacrifice, a price to be exacted for that kind of dream. The hubris of hope. The devil's backbone, a play of light and dark, of frozen movement, its beauty rooted in duty. Creosoted wood and pillars made of concrete mixed with volcanic ash carried the road to the other side. Iron bolts, overpainted and rusty, rivets, flanges, steel beams. There was nothing wrong with the bridge but the exhaustion of carrying loads. To span a crossing, a bridge had to have support. But gravity would do as it did. And descriptions didn't necessarily help you understand a thing.

Seagulls bobbed on whitecaps over a seal hunting for fry, circling a school, corralling mouthfuls of fish, stupid fish in a large silver-flecked mass: they'd escape, head out to sea, only to circle back to where they'd begun, back into danger beneath the seal.

Contemplate the horizon and the waves reflect nothing that doesn't already exist someplace.

I thought about Syd and what I would say when I got home. I'd changed from my dirty clothes into an outfit

138

bought on layaway, a leopard-skin pillbox hat and matching car coat, trying to make myself believe I'd done so for myself and not for Syd. When Juliet was young I'd put her in a nice outfit before dinner, making sure when she sat down that her hair was brushed, her nails scrubbed, that she looked every bit the princess Syd expected and not the wild girl I'd pulled from the tree and forced to wash while she screamed. Was I too harsh?

From this angle the water, a silken bedsheet, rippled by lovemaking, was knifed by a slant of sunshine. I saw all that had ever fallen from the bridge and all that would fall in time to come. The rolling surface reflected clouds, an overhanging trunk, a branch, a scatter pool of raindrops. I saw our problems as though through the lens of a telescope. Nothing had ever been so clear or so distant.

139

Closer to the water the scene became a single square inch, a green screen in front of my eye. I saw my every misstep, my every wrong turn. An eye in an eye, a little reflection of myself, my daughter, a mystery—and my failure so deep I couldn't grasp it, as tangled and jagged as a ball of barbed wire. What mattered wasn't the words to define my guilt. Only one thing mattered, and it cut through the waves with the sharp ring of a cleaver, with that clean finality, reflected in a sun of shiny steel.

At home I told Syd, "Go fuck yourself."

A couple of days went by. Two days of silent treatment.

A dog barking at nothing, soundless goldfish in a gurgling tank, dishes dirtying the sink. Images of a woman with no face came to me from time to time but like a deer on the road never stayed.

The television playing behind a closed door.

Every day Juliet invented a new way to end it all.

"I'm just going to shoot myself."

"I'm just going to drink bleach."

She complained, "I hate this place. Everyone's old."

I'd sit by the window thinking about Jameson. The good stuff. Golden. Neat. Think about the way a double warmed the throat, warmed the stomach. Soothed. I was too tired to do anything about our isolation but dwell in it, our loneliness, a house with stifling walls.

I was pulled so tight that nothing got out or in, and most days I liked being invisible—no light escaped black holes. Occasionally, though, I'd think to myself, I should smile more.

One morning a four-point buck ate the mottled leaves of potted kale plants in the backyard vegetable garden, with the casual elegance of a man at a dinner party. I'd been watching from one of the windows not boarded over, and finally, resentfully, I went out and made a hissing noise to shoo him away. He merely glanced over before taking another bite, leaves falling earthward, and if I'd been sure he wouldn't gore me with an antler I'd have thrown my slipper at him.

What did I care for kale and beets, rutabaga and turnips, all destroyed, nubs now, from the buck having furrowed a trench, nudged under the mesh and then simply stood up, splitting, with the ease of a zipper, the sturdy, eight-foot-high polyethylene? What did I care if, finished with the kale now, the buck moved to the plum tree, stretching up toward the single leaf of yellow Mirabelles I'd grafted onto the Italian blue plum tree— not because I liked yellow plums more than blue, but because it was my duty to the universe, I felt, to exhaust the possible—and balancing on his hind legs like a woman in high heels? What difference did it make? What difference did any of it make?

Road sense said you were never to swerve if you saw one. Moose, yes, deer, no. Insurance companies recommended putting a deer-warning whistle on your vehicle, and would often refuse to pay out after an accident unless you could prove you'd been using one.

The buck joined other deer clumped on a small square of salal. I surveyed the fence. Following the recommendations of the person at the hardware store, I'd sprinkled dried blood from a bag around the chicken wire. Black magic. It obviously hadn't worked.

Ron came over, emerging from the trail that connected our two properties, swinging his morning coffee in a mug that said "Porn Star." He looked at the fence. "You got the eight-foot, huh?"

I nodded.

"Yup," he said. "Yup. I told you. Gotta be at least ten."

Every week Ron was learning a new thing, diving wholeheartedly into a project or concern. Learning Russian, breeding geckos, or orchids. Meanwhile, he was the guy on the peninsula for tuna. He had his own boat, his own canning setup, his own smokehouse.

He'd gone through a phase, ate only those things he'd planted in the ground—not vegetables he'd grown but store-bought carrots, onions, potatoes; he'd bring them home, wash them, put them in the dirt, and if they grew they'd pass his safety test. Safe from what, I still wasn't sure. Now, he smiled and said he'd grab a roll of extra chicken wire from his shed.

"Be right back."

I waited, determining the strength of the posts of the deer fence that Syd and I had made from fresh-cut branches the year before, noting that they'd rooted in each corner and sprouted shoots, unwilling to be mere fenceposts, themselves in search of a purpose of their own choosing, reinforced by a spring-loaded door on the northeast side close to the house. Ron returned with a roll of fencing dragging off the rear of his backhoe, a metallic species ten feet high and more aesthetically invasive than netting.

"Really?" I said.

"It works."

"Will it at least get rusty in time?"

"Not this stuff. But if you let the morning glories go, they'll twine through it. Except that's an even bigger headache."

I admired Ron's biceps over the handle of my shovel, his perennial tan that spoke to his love of the outdoors. Pruning the posts, he whispered apologies. "These guys," he said, "link heaven and earth. Just like us. We share the same evolutionary roots. Isn't that amazing?"

Syd swaggered toward us from the back door, hands on hips, watching me in a mocking way, or maybe I was being sensitive.

"The mesh was *your* idea," I told him.

"Blame the buck. I'm innocent," he said. Then, "Juliet should be out here. What? She's part of the family. Why shouldn't she act like it?"

Ron lifted his face and smiled, gracious enough to enable the charade between Syd and me. No one said what they felt and we talked about deer instead.

twenty

Close to midnight, after Juliet had gone to bed, I received a call from Aleeki. "We're worried," he said.

My throat closed; my heart jumped. I felt a panicked squeezing inside me, a bodily labour to keep the phone in my hand and remain listening. "Why? What's happened?"

"Well, Juliet's been making posts."

"What kind of posts?"

"Oh, stuff like, What's the point of living? I hate this. I hate my life, and what's the point of it all? We thought you should know."

"Thank you," I said. "Thank you so much for calling."

Juliet had gotten much more adept at hiding her social media posts from me: none of my searches uncovered them. Nor would she accept my friend requests, insisting, "Mom, that's weird." Once again I'd respected her wishes, just the way I had when she was three and no longer wanted my kisses. And just as I had with the blood painting, the slash marks on her legs. I was trying my best; my best wasn't good enough. I was giving Juliet everything I could think of, and she was still posting things that had Aleeki concerned.

I listened outside Juliet's room. Hearing only silence, I opened the door. The room was dark; no movement came from the bed.

I gently pulled the door shut again and stood there in the hallway, alone. I went to retrieve the phone number I'd stuck to the fridge door with a magnet, a twenty-four-hour helpline. I dialed, then waited.

The woman who spoke to me was kind. I filled her in on the story, explaining that the hospital had decided to release Juliet without committing her to an in-patient psychiatric program. I detailed my frustrations, my fears, and then told her what Aleeki had said.

"I'm so, so sorry. This sounds like it's been hard for you."

The timbre of my voice must have conveyed how close I was standing to the edge, and she may have believed I was calling for myself. "Yes, it's been hard," I continued, "though not as hard for me as for Juliet. What I'm calling about now is what to do. Juliet's friends are concerned, and I'm not sure what my next steps should be."

"Juliet's in the house?"

"Yes, she's here."

"How about you let me speak to her."

"If you think that's the best thing to do. I'll go get her."

I left the receiver off the hook and ran back to Juliet's room, opened the door, less slowly this time, and approached her loft bed, where she slept on the upper bunk. The hallway light fell through the open doorway, casting a beam of light through a tunnel of black.

146

"Juliet," I whispered. "Juliet."

She was fast asleep. I began to shake her.

"Juliet, Juliet."

She opened her eyes. "What, Mom?"

"Juliet, Aleeki called to say they're worried about you."

She groaned.

"I need to ask you. What I need you to do is get out of bed."

"Why?"

"There's someone on the phone I need you to talk to. Please, Juliet, please, will you get up and do this for me?"

"Oh my God, Mom."

I insisted. And dragging her blanket behind her, she descended the ladder and followed me to the phone.

I retreated to the bathroom then, letting her talk in private to the woman on the helpline. Two or three minutes passed. I heard Juliet's low murmur, the sound, not the words, and then she hung up.

"I'm going back to bed now," she called out with a finality that put me in my place.

Had I overreacted? It was hard to tell. Given all that had come before, alarm was natural. Mired in my own confusion, I couldn't see a path forward.

The next morning I didn't talk to Syd; instead I told Ron. The part that stood out for me was the way he got up from his chair and walked around the table to put his hand on my shoulder, jolting me with static electricity.

"If you ever need a break," he said, "you know you're both more than welcome at my house, right? You and Juliet, you're both more than welcome."

"Thank you," I said, "that means a lot."

"I'm serious. Anytime at all. And hey, it'll give me a chance to practise my terrible cooking."

We did *shinrin-yoku*. Ron translated the term as "forest bathing." The sun changed shape on the mountainside. We walked the borders of his property; a skinny tree stood straight in a stiff wind next to one that had been scarred by lightning. We came across the dead doe.

Crows scattered on our approach. Nothing remained of the meat; all that was left was a skeleton, apart from a single hoof on a bent leg that looked poised to take a step, fur cuffing it like a lady with a mink sleeve.

I'd never been one to believe in signs, but on the walk back to Ron's house we stumbled across a pile of dog bones and one of several puppy skulls with bullet holes. The doe. The litter of puppies. I shuddered. Ron thought it was from the cold and put his arm around me, and I subtly recoiled from his touch even though consciously I could think of no reason my body would react this way. Something in the moment, in his touch, had made my skin crawl. I glanced at him and he smiled. Shrugging off the feeling, I noticed the dense clouds that had rolled in. As I recalled, bad luck travelled in triplicate. It began to rain, a downpour thick enough to make the mountain disappear.

We ran back to the house and towelled off. Then we sat on the couch, a tiny lantern on the table, facing each other by the front window that overlooked the pass, the gliding ferries backlighting the flowers covered in rain. Ron had pricey basalt counters. A brick fireplace. He was the kind of person who visited the Venice Biennale and who'd built his own smokehouse out of salvaged materials, including the discarded floorboards of an old famous hotel. I loved the concern Ron showed; he had the kind of eyes that seem to know a story meant a lot to the person telling it. He'd listen and offer advice, or he'd say nothing at all.

"I still hope for a miracle, a hand to swoop down and fix Juliet so that Syd and I can finally begin our lives. But what if I wait my whole life?"

"Try writing down your fears in order of importance. All those things that conspire with your insomnia. That way you can release them."

"I don't know if putting pen to paper, committing the thoughts to permanence, relieves them of their importance or increases it."

"It's a technique. Try it."

Juliet and I spent the rest of the day watching Japanese anime.

twenty-one

White urn-shaped flowers appeared on the arbutus, delphiniums grew in dry, exposed places, and yellow sheaths of skunk cabbage pushed up from swamps now filling with a sickish, sweet, springtime smell. We were still recovering from the floods, dead farm animals, cattle, chicken, mudslides, grounded barges. Syd had been out of work for a time, and so had I. Schools were closed, my postal service not taking shipments, our rail connections severed. The ferries were cancelled, we had no friends from away for Christmas. We recovered slowly from the rain and strong winds—our town still had a sinkhole—and when New Year's Day came, we bid, as a town, goodbye to a year of extremes. Mould was cleaned with bristles and buckets; people threw away mattresses, mud everywhere, the walls brown. Insurance was collected. We all helped with the volunteer relief efforts. We were still hard at work many months later. Juliet met new friends and blossomed.

Juliet started bringing her phone to the deck; she started making plans; she started staying out; she started coming home late and when asked would say nothing beyond "I was messing around with Ricky." Her laugh when she spoke to him meant everything to me. "If you can make my daughter that happy," I told him, "if you can make her laugh like that, you've changed her. I will let you see her whenever you like."

Ricky Boyd was a twenty-two-year-old who came from the oldest family on the peninsula. He was fifth generation. His people made up an eighth of the peninsula's permanent population and over a quarter of the school's. The Boyds were loggers, deckhands, bartenders, and chambermaids. They made homemade hooch from spring water and zucchinis. They also raised horses, skinny, mangy ones, and ran the delivery service, a glorified name for picking up bundles of newspapers at the ferry terminal and bringing them house-to-house in a dented minivan. A handful left the peninsula, but, like Ricky (rumour had it he'd won a million dollars and wasted it all in Nashville trying to fulfill his dream of becoming a country star), like flotsam, they always returned, unable to make it anywhere but here.

151

When Juliet met Ricky I thought, Finally, I can sleep. Finally, I can go to bed, tuck myself under the covers, close my eyes, and let go. Without hanging on tooth and nail to consciousness. Without feeling as though I'm clutching the edge of a cliff, unable to fall.

There was something apologetic and remorseful about him, like a young Syd, broken and a little afraid. And Juliet would thrive, given someone to look after. She always did her best around broken things that needed to be fixed, like bird wings, confident that she could be the one who fixed it, and there would be nothing left but to let it go, the baby crow's wing healed, its bones knitted, lifting the bird from its cage and cupping it in her hands, then opening them to the sky. It looked to me like this young man deserved our pity more than our censure.

Syd, who'd done his own time, should have been able to understand the danger of rumours, that it didn't matter what society thought of you, that you could be a good person despite having been to prison, that criminal behaviour wasn't antithetical to being a loving person, to operating with kindness.

But after all Juliet had been through, Syd was willing to rip away this small piece of happiness she'd found?

Rather than bring Ricky into our home, our hearts, rather than opening our family and making him feel part of it, Syd insisted that Juliet not see him. His baby girl.

Now, suddenly, wanting to parent. To me it felt like a declaration of war.

"You will just push them together," I said.

"Over my dead body."

"Now who's being dramatic."

Syd said, "He's a con and a meth head. The Boyds are bad. There are people you just can't be nice to, and Ricky's one of them."

"You don't know what you're talking about. Sure, he's a bit rough around the edges, but he seems harmless."

Juliet had proven that without warning she could walk out of my life, and if she ever did I might as well revoke mine. To think of a world without Juliet was not to think of a world at all. I'd been wrong to make her our battleground. She needed our support, all the nurturance I could provide. Instead she suddenly had to lie, sneak around, hide things from us. And whenever that got to be too much, she'd stop coming home for a while. Syd could have offered Ricky the kind of support that happens when one listens to another on a front porch or in a parking lot or pool hall. He could have talked to him in the language of tones, nods, and handshakes, the thousand ways a body becomes attuned to its particular world. Maybe he saw Ricky as just too much like himself. Or maybe he saw Juliet's potential wasting on the vine and it reminded him of his own wasting. No one wants to look at that.

One morning, Juliet, absorbed in her cell phone, sat on the bench that ran alongside the kitchen table. Morning cloud and a low sun. Toast and a tea, blobs of strawberry jam on a white plate.

I began to wash the floor, torturing myself with every swish of the mop, pointlessly swabbing away sticky patches. I heard the front door open. Saw Syd, upset—it was clear from his silence, his shoulders, his drawn-out sigh. He dropped a tin of coffee onto the lumber beside the door with a loud bang. "Where's my debit card?"

"What?"

He repeated the words more slowly this time, leaving large pauses between each as if speaking to a child. "I don't have it. And I don't lose things." He opened his wallet as if proving his point. "There's a lineup a mile long. Picture this. I get to the checkout but I can't pay. I look for cash but I'm two dollars short. Christ. I go out to the truck to check the cab. Finally, the cashier pulls two dollars *out of her own pocket* . . ."

"I'm sorry, hon. Where's the last place you left it?"

"In my *wallet*."

"You were with me at the store the day we bought the flour, but we used mine." I started to open the coffee with a can opener, glancing at Juliet with a "He'll take away that phone if you're not careful" look. Juliet didn't catch it, typing fast with both thumbs, her phone making little *ting* sounds in return.

"Think back," I said. "We were at the grocery store together." Syd's gaze darted around the room. Juliet popped the last piece of toast in her mouth, rose to give me a quick hug, and stood on tiptoe to kiss Syd's cheek.

"I'm heading. Peace out, parental units."

"Sit down," Syd said. The staring contest began; his glare froze her in place. "You have an obligation to this family. Sit down. I'm not done."

"I'm living with the Gestapo."

I raised my hands in surrender, pushing away the anger. "I'm not the Gestapo!"

"All you've done is switch roles." Now Juliet locked eyes with mine. "Mom, this is bullshit."

I turned to Syd. "Let her go."

"Rose," he said, rolling his eyes, shaking his head. "Rose, Rose. Rose, Rose, Rose. Whose side are you on?"

"What do you want me to do?"

"If you don't agree from now on, shut up. That's what I want."

"I put a smile on my face and do what you want?"

"Jesus. Will you two stop? Listen to yourselves," Juliet said.

Syd began ranting, then, about his uncle's baseball having gone missing. Signed. Worth four hundred dollars, with the logo.

The debit card. The baseball. The implication was clear: Ricky.

I reached for a pan on the stove, lined with a white coating of that morning's bacon fat, and threw it in the slop sink, shattering a wineglass underneath it.

"*Geez*, Mom," Juliet said, and once more made to leave the room.

"You're not going anywhere," Syd said.

"You might as well just kill me."

Juliet left the house, slamming the door behind her.

I told him, "If you wanted to parent Juliet you should have started sixteen years ago." I told him, "She's almost a woman and can make her own decisions." I told him, "We can offer advice but we can't take away her freedom to choose."

Syd lowered himself to where Juliet had been sitting on the bench, put his elbows on his knees and a palm to his forehead.

I said, "Look. Look at my struggles with Juliet and her outpatient therapy. She keeps missing sessions and the counsellor's getting frustrated. But even the law says she's allowed to decide what she wants to do with her time—no one's forcing her into those sessions. Which is *the law* telling us that Juliet has the *right to choose*, even if what she's choosing isn't good for her. Do you understand? She's an adult," I told him. "We have to let her live her own life. Let her learn natural consequences by making her own mistakes."

"Yeah, well I know for a fact that making a mistake can get someone killed."

twenty-two

When Juliet still hadn't come home by nightfall, my
nerves began to unravel again. I went to Ron's, and on
my way called Juliet, just to check in. "You going to
Ricky's? You okay? We didn't mean to fight in front
of you. I'm sorry." I paused, remembering and flinching
at the sound the wine glass had made when I'd broken it.
"Where are you?"

"Why? Does Dad want to know?"

"No. Just me."

"I'm just out and about today looking at some new
clothes for job interviews I've got lined up," she'd lied.

"That sounds great, honey." I forced a jovial tone.
"I'm so proud of you. I believe in you."

"Yeah . . ."

"What about Social Services? They have clothes, I mean, so do I, but if you don't like them . . . and a job board . . ."

Our conversation continued like a ping pong match with forced politeness over an undercurrent of mistrust.

Later, I didn't call Juliet back, although I wanted to, terribly, and stopping myself from doing so felt more painful than her annoyance with me would have, had I caved and called again. I told myself, She needs to blow off steam.

And then, nothing. Radio silence. I spent the next day at Ron's house, too, waiting for news. Syd had phoned the night before, promising to call when he found Juliet.

"She tells me one day that she wants a romantic death," said Ron. "And I'm like, yeah, but you're dead, so you don't get to benefit, but she's going on about her legend. I asked her, so what if that's how the story ends? And she says she can't sleep, she can't turn her head off, that it's like having every channel on TV blaring at the same time."

I couldn't believe she had talked to Ron about all this. And when? "Syd thinks people who are serious don't advertise."

"Well, she's thought about it and talked about it. Maybe an overdose, but she says she's not sure how much

159

to take, and she doesn't want to end up back in Emerg, and then she thought about shooting herself but decided that would be too messy and not fair to you."

It was hard to hear Ron's words. Ron, who seemed able to broach the topic as he would any other. Syd's own reluctance—or inability—to be this open with me, with Juliet, had left me feeling defeated. "I think, hell, she's a grownup, right? She deserves her privacy. Who am I to tell her what to do with her life?"

Ron laughed. "Like you have a choice? You don't, there's no choice to be made here. None at all."

I filled the moments of that long day, freeing my mind by keeping my hands busy. I decided to clean up the doe's skull. I found it in the grass, blades already pushing through its eye sockets. It was remarkably delicate, which made me feel sad and uneasy, as did all the teeth, which were intact. Holding it carefully by the socket, I brought it back to Ron's kitchen, where I poured hot water into his spaghetti pot and put it on the stove to heat. Once the water was boiling, I added the skull, along with a pinch of salt, simmered it awhile, then removed the skull with tongs and set it on a red tea towel to dry. Later I removed the last bits of sinew with my fingers, then tweezers, stopping only when the skull was as clean as a bowling ball. I placed it in a bucket three-quarters full of hot water and poured in half a bottle of bleach I'd found under Ron's sink. The smell reminded me of Juliet's infancy, diapers in a pail.

I set down the bucket on the porch step. The skull reflected the moonlight and appeared to glow.

twenty-three

I hadn't heard from Syd. I hadn't heard from Juliet. I felt gutted but didn't know what to do. I tried to call Syd. I left messages that multiplied like dead fish floating on the surface of a tank, ignored.

Ron said, "Let them be."

"What?" I was exhausted. I broke down in tears.

"For now."

In order to cope with the loss, I collapsed onto the couch. Ron sat beside me. I nestled my head into the crook of his arm. He sat silently, rubbing my shoulder. When there was no script, there was no script. His hands, I now saw, were beautiful, warm and comforting on my arm. I let myself think that everything would be okay, that choosing Ron now made everything right. We went into his laundry-strewn bedroom, its dishevelment a contrast to the rest of the house.

There were moments his body felt strange, simply because it wasn't Syd's, but there were more moments that felt easy, and I could delude myself into believing we were the perfect fit. We touched and kissed, Syd never far from my thoughts. I know I'm not wise, but I know what I've lived through. I didn't want love; I didn't want to make love; when he pulled off my shirt, I wanted to punish myself and in that instant I saw what Juliet had been running toward—not death, but that large grey area between life and death. I seemed to now be running at it full tilt, looking for answers to a desperation neither Juliet nor I knew how to express. Because I didn't want to break down in front of Ron again, I asked him to roll us a joint. He sat, his knees up on the bed, crushed a bud and put it into a glass pipe. I was a little embarrassed; he passed it to me; naked, on the bed in front of him, I suddenly felt exposed.

I stole a glance at my reflection in the mirror above the dresser—full puckered mouth, smear of red lipstick on my chin—and scared myself. Ron looked distressingly pale and thin. We were pictures of despair. Two sick people, helplessly clinging to each other. Like shipwrecked sailors. Like starving orphans. Like the weight of a body clinging to a rope by its neck.

163

My phone rang about the same time. I reached for it, scrambling off the bed and into the bathroom. It was Syd.

"Where have you been?"

I was silent, looking down at the cold bathroom tile.

"You know," he said finally, "I phoned to tell you that I was wrong. That I'd been thinking about what you said, about how there's a fuzzy line between doing nothing and doing something that could have prevented it, and knowing where that line is." A pause. "Are you even going to ask if I found her?"

"Well?"

"Well what?"

"Did you find her?"

"Do you even give a fuck?"

It felt like a smack upside the head, his implied accusation, as if I'd spent my lifetime with a stranger, invisible, unseen, since Juliet's safety was the one and only fuck I did give. I bristled, slowly moving the phone from my ear, and, in revenge, returned to the bedroom, Ron asking, "Everything all right?" nodding my head, and crawling back under the covers.

After fits and starts we found a rhythm, a sad and jagged rhythm. A person's need for food continued in times of famine, grew worse until all they could do was dream of dishes once enjoyed. My fingers read Ron's skin like a Braille love story. Because the amount of time in which I'd no longer exist stretched further than the mathematical point in which I did. Because somewhere two monkeys sat in a too-small cage, one with its arm around the other. Because somewhere a stranger was blocking the wind for someone lighting a cigarette. Because love was a fire that needed someplace to burn.

Suddenly, I sat up. "I can't. I can't." I put on my shirt. This had gone too far already.

Afterward, a shaking that started near my waist and ran like an electrical wire in both directions overcame me; at one point Ron put his arm around my shoulder and stroked it up and down. I sat there, pressed against his body, full of self-loathing, unable to escape his grasp that smelled of sandalwood. My God I was transparent, predictable, like the plot of a romance novel. Finally I lay back, convincing myself I was fine. Ron began to snore, and then I started weeping. To feel one way and live another made you a liar, at the very least. I didn't sleep. I wouldn't sleep. Not here. Sleep was too much like death.

I retrieved the doe's skull from the bucket on Ron's porch and carried it home. I set it on the kitchen table, dunked my head under water, towelled off my hair, then gazed at it, listening to the wind chimes triggering a grief that held my heart heavy the whole night long.

Only in the morning did I notice a gaping hole where Juliet's door should have been.

twenty-four

Syd told me what happened so long after he should have—by which time I'd already heard it from various people—that I accused him of conspiracy. I heard his side of the story only later, when the hard words we were launching at one another turned into a confession. Syd said, "How could you not have seen it? How could you not have known?"

"You kept crucial, life-threatening things from me," I spat. I was using outrage to hide the mounting guilt I felt, that—as all of it had been happening—I'd been at Ron's.

When Syd still hadn't heard from Juliet after he'd accused her of stealing his debit card, he had opened the front door and looked around but she wasn't sitting on the step or out in the yard. He'd gone out to look for her on the trail to the bridge, hoping he'd find her meditating off to the side of it, somewhere in the forest, but he'd had no luck and returned home. The setting sun glinted half-heartedly onto a stand of alders as Syd went back inside, sat, dialed Juliet's number. I'd gone to Ron's, leaving most of the breakfast dishes on the table. Hours later they were still there. Juliet's phone rang and went to voicemail. Syd didn't leave a message. He stacked the rest of the dirty plates and dropped them into the sink with a clatter; he saw the wineglass I'd broken and left it there.

It began to rain. *Ra-tat-ra-tat.* The downpour tumbled like a steep mountain waterfall, battering the young alders that swung in warning and hitting the roof of the converted shipping container I'd suggested we buy to replace the leaky trailer. The wind kicked up. Syd entered Juliet's room to find clues.

"I have the right—every parent does," he said, searching my eyes for validation as he recounted what happened next. What was in the house affected him, and his job was to guide her toward becoming a responsible adult. If bad things were happening, she'd need his advice more than he needed her trust.

"Don't parents have a—a duty to protect their kids from their own stupidity?"

I told him that maybe it depends on how we choose to protect them.

Then he dropped the bomb.

The room reeked of pot, the ashtrays overflowed, but worst of all, hidden behind the space heater he found a shoebox of used rigs. She was using drugs. He sat down heavily on her desk chair and closed his eyes. Once more he called Juliet, who didn't pick up, then he called all her friends, none of whom had heard from her. Syd cleaned the room from top to bottom with a dishcloth soaked in oil soap. Then he emptied her room of everything except the mattress and a blanket. The last thing he did was remove her door.

168

He guessed that Juliet was with Ricky. Despite Syd's loathing of Ricky, he and I both got what she saw in him: after a string of romances with preppie high school boys, she was returning to the land of her birth—and we both knew how much Syd and Ricky had in common. Legacies were passed down whether people liked it or not.

Syd's phone buzzed. A text message from Juliet: "Stop calling me. I didn't take your fucking debit card."

He texted back, "This isn't about the card. Where are you?"

No response. He put the phone down.

After his initial call, when he'd spat his accusation at me—*Do you even give a fuck?*—Syd hadn't tried to reach me again. Not to tell me about what he'd found in her room, not to tell me he thought she was at Ricky's, that Ricky was "hiding" her. He hadn't told me about how he'd sat for hours, then loaded bullets into his shotgun. To scare Ricky and bring Juliet home in case Ricky refused to let her go.

"So I'm telling you now," he said.

He found the rifle shells next to the Saran Wrap, sat down again, and began loading the magazine, thumb and forefinger working in Zen-like harmony.

I'd always known he liked the meditative quality of this act, had watched his fingers choosing the shell by feel from the Ziploc baggie on his lap so many times, sitting in his favourite chair. But this time was different. It was as if the rain, he told me, was somehow short-circuiting the tactile intelligence of his hands as he inserted the shells one at a time, the tip of the rounds pointed forward, and slid them into place—slide, press, click. The last time it had rained that hard, he reminded me, we'd gotten back from town to find instant noodle packages floating in the kitchen. The house had taken weeks to dry out. Back then we used to laugh.

Had I been there I would have told him to breathe, to count to ten, to think things through. I wasn't there. I called my absences his cooling-off time. He called it my being a flake.

"My God," I said. "You wanted to scare the kid with a *gun*? In front of Juliet. That's illogical."

He sighed deeply and hung his head, shutting out my words, a sign he was giving into the pressure, the anger, the fear, searching for some way to escape.

He'd needed advice, but didn't like when I was the one who dispensed it. Unlike Syd, I wasn't broken up by Juliet's infatuation with Ricky. If he'd asked me how to get Juliet back, I'd have just replied, "Back from what?"

Instead, he looked at me and said, "Okay. I've been a shitty parent. Is that what you want? You want me to say it?"

The first time she'd been out all night, "messing around with Ricky," gardening had distracted him. I'd tried to help, let the dirt distract me, too, because I thought I owed it to him to try it his way, in case he had a point about over-involvement, in case my love was really just a form of selfishness. Or self-pity. He'd hoed rows for tomatoes and beans, emptied the flats, planted the seedlings in the ground, staked them. He'd moved on to quarrying the hilly area of our property with a pickaxe, pulling up slabs of sandstone, a couple the size of Ricky's pitbull, and half-burying their shallow faces in graves around the vegetable patch. Then he'd built a stony walking trail in a loop, a circular trail to nowhere.

But that was before he knew Juliet was using again.

This time, he stood up from where he'd been sitting, loading the gun. He'd fallen off the wagon again, not a slip but a wipeout, had been drinking for hours, starting with beer and moving to whisky. He walked into the kitchen, grabbed his boots from the mat by the back door, jammed his feet into them, laces flapping, jacket, hat, truck keys, shotgun.

"Violence wasn't an answer," I said, closing my eyes.

"But who would send a man to jail for bringing his daughter home? Scaring her boyfriend a little. Maybe I could've even made good on a life that had amounted to crap. Juliet, at least, deserved to know I was finally turning into the father I always should have been."

Checking his pockets one last time, he headed outside.

He hurried down the driveway in the rain, his Mossberg 500—my favourite for its versatility and its tear-down ease—snug in its foam casing, in its pack, zipped and over his shoulder. He climbed into the truck, a '76 Chevy with stained upholstery.

He was drenched clear through to his boxers. His smokes, when he reached for them, were wet too.

I'd tried to teach him that anger wasn't good or bad in itself but more like a leopard whose cage door must be left open—the essential thing being that it had the freedom to roam. But as he spoke, I recognized a larger beast pacing uncaged: not my anger at Syd for having gotten his gun and climbed into his truck, but my own shame. While he was going through these motions—parenting, for once, in his own imperfect way—I'd been blissfully unaware that Juliet was using, that she'd tried anything beyond weed in the first place. Rather than call to tell me about the shoebox of used rigs, knowing me, knowing a phone call like that would have sent me running back to the house with worry, he'd tried to handle it on his own. The team we'd tried to be for Juliet, the gardeners side-by-side in the dirt of a vegetable patch, was falling apart in front of me. The beast turned inward, eating at me as I listened.

He started up the truck. "I convinced myself," he said, "that I was only doing what I had to do."

Syd had been to Ricky's that one time, but that had been in daylight and this was night, and he'd been sober then but wasn't now, and it was raining. He saw deer in the darkness.

Whatever he did or didn't do that night would forge Juliet's future—this he knew with the certainty of a dying man. There was no going back. In movies opportunity knocked Frank Capra–style and in real life it came when you were at the bar. In movies there were second and third chances. In real life people ate, shit, fucked, and died. No plot, no story, and certainly no redemption. Lives didn't even have proper endings. Let him go to jail. Let the whole Boyd family come after him. He felt sure

Juliet was at Ricky's, and that Ricky was covering for her. I'd once told Syd that feelings weren't facts and that you didn't have to act on them. But if you couldn't trust your gut, he'd responded, who could you trust? He felt what he felt. Nothing made sense. His baby girl had tried to kill herself.

He'd missed a turn so pulled a U-ie, narrowly missing a vehicle he hadn't seen coming. He slowed—it was the cop, Andrea; he knew her name—and then she flickered blue-red light and her siren blared twice.

She stopped him, checked his licence, and then let him off easy, saying, "Start up your truck. Don't drive like an idiot and don't go anywhere except for straight home. Do you understand?"

She followed him home in the rain.

When he'd pulled into the driveway and honked goodbye to Andrea, he took his boots off outside and left them there, as if she were still watching him. The universe had sent him a task to do; the moral agent inside him had a chance to make things right.

I thought, What moral agent?

He set off again, this time without getting lost.

At the end of the drive he found the house where Ricky lived with his mother. A large open field, the woods sparser near the front, thickening near the back where they climbed a hill with scrub brush.

173

"I left the shotgun in the passenger's seat. I was only going to go back for it if Ricky put up a fight."

Ricky opened the door.

"She's not here, man."

"You won't mind if I don't take your word for it," Syd said and walked in. Supplies were stockpiled everywhere like a freakish bunker; there was barely room to move. From floor to ceiling: cartons of toilet paper and flats of tomato soup. Boxes of surgical gloves; clear garbage bags of teddy bears, all the same; industrial-size jars of mustard, unopened packages of face cloths.

Syd entered a room where drips in the windowsill were collecting in yogurt containers. Then another, where a curtain flapped through broken glass. The rain outside sounded like water running from a tap. Ricky's mother didn't seem to be home. After looking through every room but the bathroom, he returned to the kitchen.

"Have a seat," Ricky said, grabbing Syd a beer from the fridge whose door had been spray-painted with "We don't eat, just drink" in big black letters. "I love Juliet to death, man," he blurted, "but she's fucked up."

Then a woman with a chipped tooth and a skirt so short you didn't have to imagine hard what was under it emerged from the bathroom, balancing fresh rocks of cocaine on an absorbent paper towel like tiny yellowish bits of snot. She wrinkled her nose at Syd before holding out the crack pipe.

Ricky offered him a hit and Syd declined.

"Where's Juliet?" Syd asked.

"Yeah, I think she went to the mainland to score." He held out the beer. "Come on. Take it."

Syd looked down scornfully at the bottle in Ricky's hand, said, "I don't drink," then turned around slowly and made his way out, skirting around a Camaro on blocks and narrowly avoiding the pitbull on a chain.

"You knew it, Rose. You just didn't want to see. There's no way you missed the signs, we both just ignored them."

When he finished speaking, the pieces started to come together to form a picture: a reality I wanted to shatter. Back into nonexistence. My shame rose and tore into me. He was right. How could I not have seen it? Wearing sunglasses indoors, staying in her room, the glazed look, the long sleeves. Her secrecy, her privacy—particularly about her bedroom. A privacy I'd wanted to respect, but instead became a darkness she could hide in. That is, when I saw her in her room at all, or was allowed inside: the one day a week I was permitted in, on Sundays to retrieve her laundry, always in her presence. That time I tidied her room and she said sternly, "Don't open that closet," before pivoting to something lighter, less suspicious: "It's a mess in there. I'll clean it later." The way she only opened her door a crack to stick her head out, or left her room swiftly shutting the door behind her. I'd barely given it a second thought at the time. Her drug use, Ricky, running away. All the signs and symptoms staring back at me as what they really were: just alternate methods of killing herself.

I felt the walls closing in on us, on our freedom.

"You grew up hard," I said to Syd, as gently as I could. "And I think it's made a part of you hard, deep down."

"I know how to make difficult decisions when other people would just freeze. It might mean ignoring whether it's right or wrong in the moment, but I can deal with that later."

"I've seen it." What I kept to myself was that people called that trait psychopathy.

I began to sense a truth about who Syd was, who Juliet was, slowly sinking in—avoiding, for as long as I could, what it might mean for who I was.

twenty-five

I had never considered that Juliet could lie. Back then it
was still my belief that, troubled as she was, my daughter was not a *liar*. She'd grown into a private person,
but always an honest one—sometimes brutally honest.
I knew teenagers lied, but Juliet never struck me as
needing a reason to. If Syd had come to me and told me
point blank, without the evidence of the used rigs, that
Juliet was using drugs—the exact thing I'd condemned
him for not doing—I wouldn't have even believed him.

It occurred to me later, when she sat before me at
the kitchen table, her lips set in a hard-lined grimace,
blurry-eyed, finally telling me everything, that she
might have started doing drugs—hard ones—because of
us. My stomach twisted and tightened at the thought.

Maybe our failures had pushed her to the edge, our ill-nesses inherited.

Juliet said that after we'd spoken on the phone and she'd told me she was looking for new clothes for job interviews, she had pushed her backpack down the street in a shopping cart and then parked it in an alley behind a Chinese bakery that had once given her a free steam bun because she'd learned the Cantonese word for "thank you." The aroma of soy chicken and sesame balls mingled with the smell of dumpsters and soup kitchens. She hadn't been expecting much, but volunteers ladling soup into Styrofoam cups had offered her a rare culinary experience for lunch and the kind of junkie comfort food—chocolate cakes, Twinkies—that was ubiquitous on the skids. "The last room was excellent," she said. "I'd imagined there would be a cockroach or a mouse infestation and was pleasantly surprised that despite all the alcoholics, the place was quiet."

Suddenly, it seemed to me, this girl who'd gone from wearing the uniform of the cynic, anarchy T-shirts and army boots, was lost in a dark world, and acquiring a soul through fear, not strength, in alleys, at night, watching her back, looking ahead into that space for switchblades, brass knuckles, pepper spray. Life was her elevator, starting with doubt on the ground floor. Trust lived in the penthouse; it had a view—they occupied the same building, not enemies, but lovers. A person had to go up slowly, doubt growing into trust as the floors went by. The stories she told me of fights and double-crosses made me feel this way. As far as how much she trusted me? I was starting at ground level with my most cherished. When Syd found her, Juliet was sleeping in a playground. She told me later how she'd chosen one of those big, brightly coloured plastic tunnels between wooden platforms—it was covered, waterproof, windproof, up off the ground, better than a pretend pirate ship with rigging to climb . . .

And as I listened suddenly I was right there at the bell, plunged back into Juliet's childhood to a time I'd pick her up from school, Juliet beelining for the slide, connected to a maze of those same brightly coloured tubes; seven, freckled hands, pigtails and gumboots, missing her two front teeth. Juliet, at the top of the slide, started sliding down, but midway to the bottom decided to clog the tube. She thrust a foot on either side of it, stopping her descent, plugging the line, jamming the queue. Parents tittered, their stares admonishing me, and though I shouldn't have felt embarrassment—because who cared what anyone thought—I did.

"Move," I hissed.

Juliet laughed and didn't budge.

"You're being unkind." I grabbed her waist to pull her from the tube; it was like trying to grasp a fish and hold it while it flapped. Juliet wriggled between my hands, laughing maniacally, refusing to meet my eye.

"Hey," I said. "Listen. Look at me."

"No. You look like a witch."

"Look at me."

"No."

"Let go."

"I'm enchi-li-ous!"

"Look at my eyes."

180 "No! You are a mean, mean fighting machine."

She was tough as a barnacle. Juliet's laughter grew desperate. My biceps strained. My hands were around her waist and I used my elbow to knock out her left leg. Her laughter rose into a shriek. "No! No! No!"

I lifted her free, fast-food ketchup packages falling out of her pockets. How I wished I could lift her free now.

She had kicked my shin and thrown me off balance. I'd lost my grip and off she ran . . .

I was staring at her now and she faltered in her story.

"You don't know who I am," Juliet said.

The constant and heavy darkness of her room. Occasions she'd been so tired she'd passed out in front of me, once mid-sentence. She'd played me when I questioned her. She'd lied to the doctor at the hospital, saying she'd only smoked a joint once or twice. I'd believed her. She'd duped me.

Juliet's defiant look returned. "I saw Dad around the neighbourhood, stalking me."

"Looking for you. Not stalking. We were really scared, Juliet, and I didn't even know just how scared I should have been."

I thought, she's right, I don't know her at all. Syd, meanwhile, had caught the signs but had failed to disclose them to me.

twenty-six

182   Syd told me later that when he'd found Juliet, her legs protruding slightly from the playground tube she'd slept in, he recognized her clothes—pink jeans with holes at the knees—before he recognized her, nodding off, a belt wrapped around her bicep. He took off his jacket and wrapped it around her shoulders, trapping her the way one traps a small bird. He lifted her to her feet. Juliet realized what was happening and tried to get away but was too high to fight. When a car honked and the driver unrolled his window to yell, "Get your chick in pocket," it seemed a personal warning, a signal to pay attention.

Syd threw her into the truck. "This is so easy. See? See how easy? Anybody could do this, Juliet. Anybody."

Her state that morning bore keeping an eye on. Had he drawn the right line? Or had he stepped so far over it that there was no going back?

I didn't know, myself. Before, I would have had answers for him, but now I was searching desperately for my own answer to how it all began, as with the suicide attempt. The only time I could get away from the all-consuming job of looking for those answers was when I was with Ron. I could only escape the act of blaming myself, of keeping a meticulous inventory of my parenting mistakes, by pulling away, leaving the house, going to Ron's. Only away from my house could I confront the truth that my problems with Syd, our problems with Juliet, had become so large, so unwieldy, that I couldn't fix them. As soon as I released my self-blame, I released my control. Only at Ron's could I allow myself to feel powerless.

Syd claimed he'd have given Juliet money to start a new life if he hadn't thought she'd spend it on drugs. He'd never been physical with her before. He'd never had to manhandle her—he'd never even believed in spankings the whole time she was growing up, and now he had to ask himself where the line between help and harm had gone.

He couldn't remember the last time he'd felt awake. When he couldn't sleep, I'd often suggested ocean sounds.

If they'd made Sleep Sounds of an idling diesel 350, he'd have listened to that all night long. His half-dream limbo blurred the boundary between hero and villain and the fatal mistakes between the two.

184

twenty-seven

I awoke in my own bed, after returning home from Ron's the night before, shocked by the sun's angle through the curtains and pushed off the blanket that had been thrown over me during the night—I'd fallen asleep with no recollection of having done so, all my clothes on, on top of the bedspread. The silence of the house filled me with a deep sense of unease. I rubbed my eyes, blocking out the dull morning light, the rumpled bed I'd tossed and turned in all night. I didn't know what more I could do. What Juliet's counsellor had said haunted me: "Some people will kill themselves no matter what intervention takes place."

I wanted to believe Juliet was crying wolf, still told myself so, especially now that I had no control over the situation. At the same time I felt the cruel brutal guilt of realizing that, if I got *the* news, part of me would be relieved: Juliet wouldn't be disappointed or unhappy anymore. Then a deeper revelation: part of me was tired. And I hated myself for it. For being weak. I wanted to go back to sleep. Some days that's what I wanted more than anything. Other days I'd rather do nothing at all.

I climbed down from the loft bed and went out into the hallway. That's when I noticed the empty doorway where Juliet's door had been removed from its hinges. Before I could question it, I heard a sound and turned.

Ron came down the hall, coffee in one hand and breakfast in the other, two eggs and toast. He urged me to eat. Not even wondering what he was doing in my house, I returned to the bedroom numbly, a robot following instructions. I drank the coffee, dark and strong, while Ron sat on the end of the bed, staring off into the middle distance as if it hid answers to mysteries he'd been seeking. Or maybe he too was tired and numb and was staring at nothing at all. The perfect pair of easy-over eggs on my plate, their rich yellow yolks melting inside my mouth like an elixir, helped calm me, but not for long.

"Take the morning for yourself," Ron said. "Go to the farmers' market or get your hair done. You deserve it. I'll hold down the fort." He meant well, was trying to stitch a wound.

But the thought that Syd had sensed the shift in me—*Do you even give a fuck?*—made me anxious, his instinct like a seismograph that senses shifts in the earth's tectonic plates.

I did not go shopping or get my hair done.

As a former stuntman, often consulted on shows, Ron had access to wonderful things used during filming and now discarded. This is how he ended up with, for example, a pallet of plastic dolls, of all things, and I'm ashamed to say that on that day I took a number of them up into the hills. I borrowed Ron's 4x4 and drove up logging roads with a backpack full of bullets and a couple of small-bore rifles, turning off onto dry creek beds, driving farther, tires spraying pink granite into rock-solid ruts. Dried mud in the clearing. I stood in the dark presence of another's targets, red cloth strips fluttering in branches, and proceeded to arrange my own. Babies of all sizes, toddler dolls that could stand if you balanced them properly. I set them up in the trees: babies everywhere. Sniper-like, I aimed and shot each one in the head.

What stood out wasn't the rifle's kick, or the scattering of sharp-shinned hawks, or the field mice they'd been circling. It wasn't the rifle's clack, or the grace with which the barrel and buttstock could be joined without tools, the simplicity with which they could be split in two. That struck me, a powerful metaphor, and on the drive home the thought of it kept leaping out at me like a deer on the road, dangerous, transfixing, along with other thoughts that had lately not left me alone. But what stood out? The puff of smoke through the scope, the baby disappearing from the limb of the tree.

twenty-eight

I knocked and then let myself in. "Ron?" I called. I left my muddy boots at the back door and hung my windbreaker on the hook. Ron walked toward me, his arms ready for an embrace. He hugged me. My back ached for a hot shower. A moment of awkwardness followed. The stillness felt off, the sun trapped between window and curtain. A morgue-like silence had settled in. I took a step, he tried to sidestep, we ended up going in the same direction and then doing that little dance that betrayed nervousness even as it tried to hide it. He let out a laugh. Self-conscious. We stumbled out of the doorway and down the hall.

I sat on Ron's couch and dialed Juliet's number; it went straight to voicemail. So did my call to Syd after one ring.

Ron sidled up next to me, slipped his arms around my waist, peeked over my shoulder. "Anything wrong?" He touched my hand gently before I slid out of his grasp and found myself on the verge of tears, my entire body saying, Stop. All I wanted was everything to hold off long enough for me to get my wind back. I saw exhaustion in the lines of Ron's face. The exhaustion said, What now?

"I still can't reach her. I'm calling 911."

He put a hand on my shoulder. "Really?"

"I just can't get over the feeling that something really bad has happened."

He left the room. I called the police and was directed to Andrea. "Juliet is missing."

She asked me to remind her how old Juliet was.

Meanwhile, Ron was banging around in the kitchen.

"Sixteen."

"Sixteen," Andrea repeated. "You said her father left to find her?"

"Yeah, but I told you. I can't reach her."

"Have you tried calling her father?"

"What do you think?"

She paused.

"Tell you what. I'll take down her phone number. We'll call and make sure someone checks in with her. Then we'll move on from there. Rose, listen, okay? I know you're hurting."

"I feel like you're going to tell me it's hard to let go. Or that birds fall out of the nest when they're learning to fly." I let this platitude hang in the silence like air from a punctured tire. "Look. Don't patronize me."

"Make yourself a cup of tea."

I hung up. I didn't make tea. I left Ron. I left him standing at the door, wondering what the hell was wrong with me.

Syd's irrigation tools were hanging on the garage wall next to Juliet's mountain bike. I got into my car, feeling an immediate need to get away from the source of my pain. Get out, get out, get out. My feet needed to run.

I drove around to look for her as if I knew where to go. Karma needed to slap upside the head those who deserved it. Wrongs needed to be righted, harmony restored. I drove too fast, skimming past overgrown fields, gated driveways, looming hills. I crossed over a grey canal, half-thinking I should hit one of the lodgepole pines on the side of the road. A demon had taken over—I wasn't driving so much as passengering, being led, but to where? I didn't know.

It was instinct. I jumped as if the car were on fire. I jumped because I had to get out. Because something had to get out. Because it hurt. Because of the flames, except there were no flames. How many men had I loved and escaped? How many had let me down? Always a hitch, a clause.

I was just trying to get out of the damn car. Seatbelt off, ground moving, door open. I pulled over then, helpless. I leapt toward the grass, wet and long and green, moving in the space between the open passenger door and the frame of the car. Leaning into the air—thin air, the air moist and green, the grass long, the deerfoot spreading in the ditch—leaning into thin air, I fell. I got back up. Dogs barked beyond the trees—someone would sic them on me, the runaway. Call the police. I ran, I ran through trees. Dogs barked—I was a bear, a cougar; nothing hurt my feet. Nothing hurt, because I ran. Ran, ran, and then, and then I tumbled. I squatted and frogs croaked; then I ran between two fences. Dogs barking. I should take my time, I thought. I didn't know where I was. I didn't know where I was, a relative term: I was here. I was here, I was here. I was old, I was sick, I was shitty but here I was. Back at the car. Full circle.

I screamed. I kicked the tire. I slid down the car and came to rest on the highway. A pain radiated up in my heart, enough to double me over. A gut punch that felt like heat, guilt pangs round and rolling as a river. Tears in the rain and a roundness in my belly, the labour pains of swallowed stones. My jeans soaked through.

I breathed in and out like a runner, not feeling the cold. No one gave a shit except about themselves. The country was burning. I could die. Maybe then I wouldn't care. The hole was always growing, not knitting itself like a broken bone. Like a knuckle smashed once, I didn't know how to stop breaking. No finish line but this, a road, pavement. I slammed my head backward. Once, twice. I screamed at the sky. The wind rose and fell, singing a song of grief, the oldest song the world knew.

I arrived home cold, wet, hungry. A message awaited me on the landline. I returned the call. Then Andrea's voice telling me, "Juliet's fine. She's not suicidal." I listened silently to her explain that she'd phoned and had done a wellness check herself.

"I'll tell you this, she's with Syd. She's with her father. Okay? They've just brought a blanket to the shore along the old bay road. They've got a fire going, and will be spending the night there."

What did I expect? That Juliet would run into Andrea's arms and say, "Take me to my mom"? Then Andrea's words sunk in: the shore, the fire. "What day is it?"

Andrea hesitated at the odd question before answering, and when she spoke it dawned on me that it was the day Syd's uncle had died. This was his tradition. Every year on this day, he brought roses to the shore to mark the anniversary. My relief that Syd had found Juliet was quickly eclipsed by my anger at him for not taking her straight home—an anger that would triple in size when I learned later about the drugs, about where and how he'd found her. Instead of bringing her home, he had scooped her up into the car, driven to a grocery store to get the roses, and then taken Juliet, still high, with him to the shore to make a bonfire and camp out for the night.

Parking the truck in the bend of the bay road where arbutus and cedars tangled, Syd told me later, he negotiated the steep path to the ocean with the flowers and when he reached the water's edge he put the flowers in one by one. Some of the roses floated out to sea, some sank, and some returned to the spot where he stood next to Juliet, fallen into a slump on a log with her hands crossed tightly over her chest and hidden from view, her head down, subdued now, at least for the moment. When these stems grazed the toe of his boots, wet from the bay's small lapping tongues, he wasn't sure what to do. He could pick them up or leave them. Neither seemed right. It bothered him the whole time he was building a fire: that the roses had floated out then changed their minds. That they'd come to rest, bobbing next to his shoe print in the sand. The guilt I felt for forgetting the importance of this day gave way to the worry I felt for Juliet, my longing to be with her. I was jealous of their collusion, their maladaptive bond.

"Basically, he's kidnapped her?"

"To take her so that you can have a break. So that she can have a break. It's not a kidnapping if she wanted to go."

I hung up. I paced, unable to concentrate on any one thing. The thought that I was driving Juliet to despair grew louder. My head was like a cageful of birds, beating their wings, shrieking. My head was an angry choir that told me what to do. I cut, poked, and pinched. I knifed, burned, chewed, scissored, scratched my arms with my fingernails. I punched drywall and broke a hole in it, leaving my fist swollen and bleeding. I sat down and watched myself burn like a candle the wind kept blowing out, returned to relight myself, flame to my wrist. I needed to teach myself a lesson. It was the only way I'd learn. Was Syd doing this—keeping Juliet—to protect her? From me?

195

Jaw clenched all night. Grinding, grunting in my sleep. Because I couldn't fight. Because I'd have broken the passenger window with my fist. Because I'd have had to strike. Because the no-flames tried to kill me. Because I was weak then. Because I'd been broken long before. Because all you could control were your own impulses.

Because you couldn't make others do your bidding. Because it was wrong. Because it assumed that we possessed the insight to know what was good for another creature.

I had to get my head straight. What the fuck? Why, why, why couldn't I deal?

Could anyone?

A voice seemed to reply, Loyalty to yourself, baby.

But it's not on them, I argued, it's on me. Trust is stupid, loyalty is stupid. And I'm not a fucking baby. I hate this head trap. I want to rail and be held by a pair of arms but there were no arms except those that made me want to escape.

I wanted out, I wanted in. I was a cat that couldn't make up its mind—in, out, in, out.

Maybe I was a siphon. A channel from the universe, a conduit for suffering to teach others. I was scared in high places: I'd look up and grow dizzy. The height. And the ease with which anyone could kill themselves from up there. That was the thing. I couldn't fly. I wanted to.

twenty-nine

Syd's truck roared into the driveway in a backwash of gravel smoke, Juliet in the passenger seat. I ran out as Syd was pulling her down from the cab, grasping her elbow, walking her toward the house. "You didn't think to call when you found her?" I asked Syd. "Why are you banding against me?"

Marching her through the front door now, Juliet shouting, "I'm going to call Social Security on you!"

"You mean Services?" Syd said. He sat her down on the couch. "Don't move."

I was ready to rage against him. My fist was still swollen and throbbing, but I wanted to drive it into his throat, scream at him for not bringing her straight home, cry with relief that she was back in my scope again, sitting there on the couch. Then Syd looked at me and I felt something fall apart. I looked at Juliet and her eyes were glazed and avoiding mine.

"Let's talk," Syd said, motioning to the kitchen table. And he told me everything. The rigs, the playground. He spoke, Juliet spoke. I collapsed inside myself, crumbling like a city built atop the ruins of another. I sank through descending layers of pain, guilt, shock. Not only did I not trust our daughter anymore—I didn't recognize her. Finally, Syd stood and walked Juliet to her bedroom.

"What are you doing?" I asked.

"I'm trying to help her."

He ordered me to guard Juliet while he rehung her bedroom door. I did, standing in the hallway beside him, confused and against my better judgment as he put in screws, a lock on her door from the outside. He did the same to her window. Juliet now yelling, "This is illegal," and "I have to go pee, you fuck."

"Christ almighty." Syd went to the kitchen and grabbed a cooking pot (the same one she'd vomited in) and two bananas. "Here's a pot to piss in," he said, throwing it in, then he threw in the bananas and slammed the door. Still dazed, I handed him the screws to shut Juliet in.

"You can't keep her in there. You can't hold her hostage."

He ignored me. Soon his truck was pulling out of the driveway; he'd screwed his finger along with the door and needed medical help. Then silence pervaded.

I told Juliet, "I'm going to get you out of there, hold on."

I ran over to Ron's and spewed words (from the heart where drama lived but) that felt true: "kidnapping," "hostage." He took my hands, he made me sit, he slowly repeated back to me a complete version of what I'd said. This was Ron. Systematic, in charge. He held my hands on his lap. He looked prepared for anything.

Within fifteen minutes he'd opened Juliet's door using Syd's power drill. After letting her out, he screwed the door shut again.

Juliet was still visibly coming down off the high. She was shaken, tired, and smelled like woodsmoke from the fire Syd had made the night before. She went to hug me when Ron freed her from her room, but then stopped herself. "Mom, I need a walk," she said. "I need some air. Just some space to think. Maybe I'll visit Aleeki. But I'll be back before dinner, I promise. Okay?"

"Juliet, no. You just got back."

She hesitated. "Okay. I just need some water."

Then, when I entered the kitchen, she was gone again, had disappeared again, had left me feeling helpless. Again.

Meanwhile the doctor had cleaned, stitched, and bandaged Syd's finger, and given him a prescription for antibiotics. By then Ron and I were back at his place— I'd begun frantically calling Juliet. When there was no response, I texted her to let her know she could come to Ron's, too, that it was safe for her there. Syd returned to a silent, dark, and empty house.

I imagined he checked the screws on Juliet's door. They held fast. I imagined he thought she was sleeping, safe as a canary in a cage that he himself had screwed shut.

Then his phone rang. Juliet wasn't sleeping. Juliet was on the bridge.

thirty

Syd got to the bridge just as Ron and I did—in his truck,
his finger bandaged, confusion and suspicion in his eyes.
"What did you do?"

And there was Juliet, Andrea by her side, her cruiser
parked nearby, the two of them quietly talking.

Juliet hadn't gone to Aleeki's; she'd gone straight to
Ricky's. I should have known.

Then from Ricky's she'd made her way to the bridge,
past the church; she'd been seen walking between the
gravestones that faced the hillside, among the purple
calendulas flowering on the trail to the strait as they did
that time of year. Juliet had been leaning on the railing of
the bridge, her back to the water. She was thought to have
been acting peculiar. A call had been made to the police.

She'd been standing on the bridge, she'd later say, standing there, not thinking of jumping. She could see across the bridge to the water on the distant horizon where everyone was doing what they enjoyed, kayaking, kitesurfing, making friends, falling in love. Her father had confined her and the bridge had called; she was trying to breathe deeply, to let the beauty of the day sink into her.

Juliet's face changed when she saw us rushing toward her. She yelled at Syd, "I hate you."

Andrea stepped forward, held us back, spoke quickly. With no mental health services on the peninsula she could arrange for Juliet to visit with the locum, if she wanted; the local doctor was away.

I tried to argue for an immediate psychiatric committal.

Andrea shook her head. "The only way I could take her in right now is if she had warrants."

"You're saying that if my daughter had committed a crime the law could help me?"

It struck me once more that if Juliet were to get any help it wouldn't be from the system.

Andrea raised her shoulders in a helpless gesture.

"We'll take her home then," I said.

"I'm not going anywhere with you guys," Juliet announced, looking straight at her father.

"I'll take her to my place, okay?" Ron said suddenly. "While you two figure stuff out."

I reached around Andrea, touched my hand to Juliet's arm, a touch at last, my baby girl. I looked into her eyes, held them steadily in mine. "You want to go to Ron's?"

She groaned, shrugged. "Whatever."

Whatever—it was close enough to a yes—and this may have been the moment I began to imagine I was in love with Ron. To imagine that his way of saying he loved me back was by taking on more of Syd's role by the day.

Later Juliet would tell me that at Ron's she'd taken a bath and put on the clean T-shirt and track pants he'd given her, that she'd let him drape a blanket over her shoulders and give her a rum toddy, that she'd told him, "I wish my brain would stop" and "I wish I could be nobody because if I was nobody I'd have no worries."

He'd said he felt all alone in his head, too—is that what she meant?

"I mean," she'd said, "I have a dream to make a fresh start."

Yes, I thought. She told me the story, where on the other side of the railroad tracks the trestles stopped completely and fell into the ocean, green as far as the eye could see.

thirty-one

I decided to go talk to Ricky myself. My knuckles were red and swollen; on the way I straightened my fingers then closed them around the steering wheel again, each movement bringing a jolt of pain. In the driveway a woman, his mother, plucking dead geranium leaves.

I called out the window. "Where's Ricky at?"

"He's in the back having lunch."

I turned in, continued along the driveway by the side of the house, and there—under an old truck canopy on stilts in front of a homemade shed—Ricky stood, holding court between two young men with thin bodies and meth mouths, one picking a sore on his cheek and cleaning his teeth with a pocket knife, the other doing bicep curls, repeating "Fucking rad, bro" to Ricky as a pitbull clung with his teeth to the weight bar.

A rusty swing set with a soiled rug hanging over it leaning at a wonky angle, broken Big Wheel toys and cigarette butts littering the grass, the smell of woodsmoke mixing with sea air. Laundry dried on a fence as chickens ebbed and flowed and horses pushed toward an uncertain boundary of scrub brush on the hill like dusty whiskers on a face.

Ricky, surprisingly, hopped into my passenger seat and directed me toward the drag strip—it had been hidden by the long grass; now I could see cars shining like rare insects, here a fender, there a rear end—that led in turn to a demolition derby track where another vertebral column of crushed vehicles balanced one atop the other. A pregnant woman wearing a faded pink T-shirt that said "Bridesmaid" was relaxing in a lawn chair in front of an open car trunk filled with jars of eighty-proof at five bucks apiece. Ricky hopped out and grabbed a tote bag from its backseat. Then he threw it onto my passenger seat, in the space he'd just occupied.

"What's this?"

He looked confused. "I thought you came to get her stuff."

"This is Juliet's?"

"Yup. Pretty sure that's all of it." He paused. "I'm sorry, okay? But Syd paid me a visit and, uh . . . It's just not worth it, okay?"

I avoided looking at the bag in the seat next to me. I understood what it meant now.

I drove back home, knowing now that Ricky had broken her heart. And that if anything happened to Juliet as a result I had only Syd to blame.

thirty-two

That evening Ron phoned Syd to propose that he take Juliet out on his tuna boat.

"Three weeks on the old salt chuck," Ron said. "Give you guys a break. Exhaustion works wonders on depression."

He agreed right away: sea air, hard work were just what she needed.

I wasn't so sure. I took the phone from Syd and said, "But she'll be on the *ocean*. She could jump overboard."

"I'll handcuff her to me when I sleep if I have to," Ron said, using the same tone of voice he used when he'd asked me, "Does it feel good, Rose?"

"Rose," he said into the silence. "I *promise* I'll take care of her."

thirty-three

I spent the next few days trying to get help for Juliet. In Syd's mind it was only a matter of time before social workers and then police would be knocking on our door, all as a result of my efforts. His fear was that Juliet would be taken away—and I had to admit I could see his point.

Her Project Life counsellor, I learned, had "disenrolled" Juliet from the program. Juliet had stopped attending sessions altogether, she told me, and since she needed to be "fully participating in her own journey toward her own mental health," it was "currently impossible" to offer her further services.

"But it's your *therapy* that wasn't working," I said, barely controlling my voice.

"People think therapy will work like an antibiotic on an infection," she replied calmly. Be patient, she added; change was measured in millimetres, imperceptible to the naked eye.

How much longer could I tread water, clutching at only the vague promise that tomorrow Juliet would feel differently? "Have you known people who've been where she's been and then wanted to live?" I asked her.

"Yes, absolutely," she assured me, but I had only her words as proof.

She was terribly sorry, there was nothing more she could do.

It felt to me that bureaucracy had replaced compassion in a job where compassion meant everything. If there is any evil that remains in me, and I'm certain there is, part of it has to do with my feeling that this woman wasn't sorry at all.

At the end of each stressful day I'd clean the house. Make dinner. Forcing myself to keep busy as a way to control my rising fury.

Meanwhile we couldn't let go of the old fights, Syd and I, confrontations between us so oft-repeated they'd worn a path in our minds—like old wagon wheels, tracks made in mud. Mostly, though, we just went through the

209

motions, words staying on the surface like water spiders skittering to and fro.

"Do you want peas with that?"

"The light bulb's gone out."

My body didn't betray my affair. Not even when I crawled into bed and Syd would wrap his arms around me. I didn't lean in; I didn't pull away. His arms felt the same and my body felt the same next to his.

It was hard to be apart from Juliet, out there somewhere on the ocean. I knew it was for the best; I knew it was temporary. I tried to tell myself it was only a matter of time.

thirty-four

Juliet's three weeks on the tuna boat finally went by and she returned, tanned and healthy, regaling us with tales of seasickness and showing us her roped-burned hands.

Relief. I could feel a slight lessening of the fear that had held me in its grip. And now I wanted to renew my connection with Ron.

I wanted happiness to begin.

I went on long walks, hiking miles and miles along the river. If my shoes got wet, I'd just take them off, tie the laces together, sling them around the back of my neck. I wandered alone. I stopped making Syd dinner. Our marriage had never been at a lower point and yet I felt myself growing stronger every day, walking the river, walking the hills.

At the hoedown late that summer, Juliet, shy, panicky, told me she might be pregnant. The smell of earth in places rotted by floodwater on the breeze.

Where we lived, the hoedown—traditionally an annual celebration for farmers, the time when one put one's "hoe down"—had begun years before as a backyard barbecue. A few friends, a couple of guitars around a campfire, had turned into a music festival with an underground reputation: an event, with a stage set up on a large property where musicians could gather and play. Fake tumbleweeds, lights, sound system, multiple bands, a clearing where out-of-towners could camp. A whole pig would be put on a spit, the pig paid for by the host, who also supplied tables to vendors. A lot of drinking was involved. Locals brought dishes to share: steaming potatoes, corn on the cob, an array of desserts. We'd go every year.

This year we arrived separately and yet we all sat together, at a long table with eight or ten others, Syd, Ron and I, and Juliet. Juliet seemed peaky to me; I was watching her for signs. Syd wore a cowboy hat and I a country shirt with satin piping and pearl snaps. I brought blackberry pie and a salad.

Juliet accompanied me to the vendors' tables. A woman asked if we wanted our chakras read; we looked at pottery. "I might be pregnant," she said.

On hearing these words, several thoughts occurred to me simultaneously. One: Ricky. Ricky and his Telecaster guitar. She was seeing him again. Ron had allowed her to do so behind our backs and Ricky had gotten her pregnant.

Two: I would raise the baby.

Three: We had to keep this from Syd. I looked around nervously. Children were running wild, raising Cain. "Maybe they could give those kids a bath," I could hear him telling Ron from where we stood, "and quit breast-feeding the four-year-old, and for chrissakes make them wear some clothes in public?"

I turned back to Juliet. I didn't ask, "Who's the father?" Nor did I ask, "Are you thinking of keeping it?" We were still dealing in hypotheticals.

"Have you taken a test?"

"No, I've been scared to."

"How late are you?"

"A couple of weeks."

I breathed a sigh of relief. "Okay. Okay, it's still early then."

"I'm not sure what to do."

"Have you told the father?"

"No."

"Have you told anyone besides me?"

"No."

"Okay, let's keep it that way for now. The first thing you have to do, though, is get a test so we know what we're talking about."

She groaned. "I know, I know, I know."

"If you want, we can go to the store right now."

"What do you mean? Just leave?"

In a town where everyone knew everyone, everyone knew everyone else's business, too: a pregnancy test would make people talk. "Well, people might assume it's me . . ."

She considered this a moment. "No, don't worry about it. I'll go to town, I'll do it myself." "Going to town" meant going to the city, an hour's drive.

Juliet seemed crushed by it all. I took her in my arms and gave her a hug. "Don't worry. You're only late. It's probably nothing."

She cried a little, then wiped away her tears. "Yeah, you're probably right."

I picked out a couple of beeswax candles from one of the vendors and showed them to Juliet, tipping one under her nose. "Smell. Aren't they lovely?"

Parents drank; children ran among the trees, playing tag, climbing to the highest branches they could and clambering back down again. This year the host had set up a television in the forest for them, an extension cord leading to the plug in his shed. A few kids watched, their faces illuminated by flickers.

Someone, drunk already, pushed more wood into the bonfire with a mini track Bobcat.

Ricky played his Telecaster as he crooned Hank Williams-esque songs. He had the outfit, anyway. A flamboyant suit of gold lamé with chain-stitch embroidery and matching boots. I watched to see whether he met Juliet's eye; caught him glancing warily in our direction.

Syd was scary, a warrior, and a warrior was never more powerful than when defending his family, than when defending his daughter—I got it. The atmosphere was tense overall: Syd and I, pretending to be the couple the town expected; Ron, joking around, winking at Juliet and saying, "So it's beer and boys for you now, hey?" even though she wasn't even drinking a beer. I clocked the pop in her hand instead of a Kokanee and filed this away.

A young woman at our table was talking about a new venture in chutneys and preserves made with "all natural ingredients."

"Like arsenic?" Syd said and laughed.

"Like venom?" Ron echoed.

I rolled my eyes.

The woman looked away. Syd jerked his thumb at her and her boyfriend, then mimed armpit hair. "His hair's longer than hers," he whispered. "Unless you count that shit under her armpits. Christ. What the fuck's wrong with this generation?"

In a joking way I said, "Stop it." I meant, "You asshole."

Ron said in a low voice, "I respect a woman who feels confident enough not to shave."

I took hold of his hand and squeezed it. "*Thank* you."

Juliet shuddered.

Ron put his hand on my lower back. I lived for those little moments of electricity. I'd never meant to hurt Syd, but every time I thought of how close I'd come to losing Juliet, I knew only that I could not continue.

By eight-thirty most young parents had stopped drinking; by nine they'd collected their dishes; by nine-fifteen they'd successfully corralled their children and were ready to go. I hadn't expected Juliet to sit with us the whole night; naturally she wanted to be with friends. I was happy that at least she'd eaten with us, and now that she'd had her fill of the roasted pork and potatoes and salad she was headed toward them. Her girlfriends stood, all made-up and giggling, this group that I'd seen grow up, that seemed so like women, or at least the women they would become, but that could often seem like the children I remembered from a decade before.

Her friends were loud and I figured they'd been drinking, even if Juliet hadn't. Now they all moved to the

216

makeshift dance floor; it was just a patch of dirt in front of the homemade stage, but they hooted and hollered as if they were in a nightclub. I was happy to see them having fun. We started with one shot. Just one, we said, bowing at the host's insistence. I watched us sliding off the rails like a train, pushed ahead by the weight we towed behind us, toward moral destruction. Some days, when we fell off the wagon, we seemed more willing to throw everything we'd worked for and everything we cared about into the trash bin, irreplaceable things, precious things, family, home, reputation, self-respect. Some days the urge to drink was too hard to resist. Some days we were weak. Tempted, we surrendered, and drank like fools.

By this point Syd's wasted mission was to drink Ron under the table.

In many ways, Syd had stayed sixteen. Having spent his formative years in prison meant he'd never experienced teenagerhood and all its rites: getting a driver's licence. Acid trips. Bush parties, vehicles parked in a circle around a firepit, shining their headlights into the centre. House wreckers. A feeling of being in love with one's own freedom. Death happened to others who drank too much, drove their car off a bridge, played games involving a cherry picker removing the safety helmet from one's head, a tree falling wrong. Death happened in stories. "Had his guts squeezed out his tail end when a log rolled on him."

Meanwhile I, too, full of rancour, let myself cut loose a little too much. Keeping up with the boys, as if it evened some score. But when I began to feel queasy, I got to my feet and murmured that I'd like to go.

"I'm getting tired myself," Ron said, and offered to drive me home.

Syd flashed me such a look that I sat back down.

"Let's make a night of it then," Ron conceded.

What came next was a lesson in why we should never drink; alcohol brought out the worst in us—we felt on top of the world, poised, forcefully intelligent, charming, but the reality we couldn't see: booze exaggerated only our flaws and weaknesses.

By the end of the night only hardcore stragglers remained: middle-agers with substance abuse problems but respectable jobs—weekenders, mostly—along with a handful of locals.

Syd twisted up a joint and offered it to Ron to light.

Ron took a single toke and, not long after, passed out upright in his chair.

Syd took advantage of the moment by roughly shaking his shoulder. "Hey. Sleeping Beauty. Hey. You can't crash here."

Ron got up from the ground where he'd toppled over,

straw in his hair. We watched him make his way to his truck and fall asleep straight away behind the steering wheel. Syd collected me in his arms and spilled me into the passenger seat of the truck. He looked for Juliet, couldn't find her. She has her licence, I told myself, and would surely drive them home if Ron couldn't.

The truck began moving; I vomited out the window. I vomited again at home, then stumbled to our bedroom and fell asleep tangled in my purse strap, my running shoes still on.

The next morning I lay in bed, hungover. The only remedy (for the headache, the woozy stomach, the regret, the depression that was sure to follow) was to get up. To do what needed doing. If I didn't, guilt would only worsen the pain. And once you allowed yourself the liberty of feeling your inner sickness, like a leper looking at her sores you might never be able to look at yourself again. My worst nightmare? Not living up to my own expectations.

Juliet was at the forefront of my mind. I debated whether I should phone her, wondering whether she might have already picked up a test.

Syd snored in bed, a line of drool between his mouth and the pillow. I lay my hand between his shoulder blades as if judging the waters, watched it rise and descend with the rhythm of his breath, and decided I'd let him sleep it off.

I didn't put coffee on; I didn't even leave a note. I just threw a hoodie over my T-shirt, stepped into my flip-flops, sped out the door, and got into the car—a way to sneak up on myself, knowing that if I took my time I might not go at all.

I headed to the city, a tightness in my back. When my heart began racing, I gripped the steering wheel, making myself loosen one finger at a time, using every trick in the book to calm down. Fake it till you make it. The sooner I dealt with it the better. I bought two pregnancy tests; it would be a cliché to say I breathed a sigh of relief, and what's more it wouldn't be true.

I stopped at a gas station, filled up, and bought a coffee the colour of dirty toilet water (hot though, and caffeinated). Then, sipping the coffee on my way back home, I breathed. I felt a slow release, a loosening between my shoulders.

I was desperate to know how Juliet was doing, but she was still staying at Ron's. To pop in on her would create unnecessary drama, I said, trying to coach myself. Syd had gotten into my head with his talk of my catastrophizing. But the battle raged within me. I'd left too early to see how she'd fared the rest of the night, and for this I felt guilty, too. I asked myself why I'd drunk so much in the first place, a question whose answer lay behind layers of obfuscation. How was it that I struggled with something this basic—even when the stakes were so high they could get no higher? Even when I could stand to lose everything? I cross the line, enter the gap. I parked, got out of the car, brought my coffee into the house. I looked into our room and saw that Syd was still in bed, curled around his pillow.

I went into the garage and rummaged frantically to find my emergency pack of smokes. Finally, out on the back porch, I lit a cigarette and called Juliet. Voicemail. Not knowing what sort of a message to leave, I hung up.

Then I called back. This time I was ready for the beep, but Juliet answered. And although I didn't want to push, I knew I had to. "Want to have lunch?"

A pause.

"What about I pop by with coffee? I went into town this morning." I walked down the path toward the gate. "It's going to be okay, okay? I promise it's going to be okay."

"Yeah."

"So, can I come?"

"I don't know, let me call you back."

"Okay," I said. And then, before she hung up, "But don't wait too long."

I hopped into the shower and tried to occupy myself, taking the washing of my hair very seriously. I couldn't call her back and hurry her along. Covering every portion of my scalp with suds, I willed time to pass. I rinsed until every strand squeaked and then soaped every inch of my body, every inch, and shaved with the concentration of a woman on her way to be judged. I already felt I was treading on dangerous ground. I brushed my teeth, once, twice, and chose my clothes with the deliberate care of a person going to a wedding or a funeral. I grew more anxious every minute. Talking to Juliet had become difficult. I was never sure how she'd take what I was going to say, never sure whether I'd be pushing her into a place of desperation simply by trying to help. The walking-on-eggshells feeling, Syd called it.

My phone didn't ring. I peeked through the deciduous trees and salal that separated the two houses. A hunter, scanning for movement. Every time a bird flew from a branch I noted the motion and my heart soared, thinking it was Juliet moving through the trees, only to have my heart sink back down.

Maybe waiting for her call was the wrong thing to do. Maybe I should phone. Maybe she was interpreting my reluctance to push as the withdrawal of love. It was hard to know. Stuck in limbo, I stared uselessly at the phone in my hand, willing it to ring, thinking hard about Juliet so

222

that she'd think of me. "Phone, phone, phone, Ju-liet."
A mantra. My eyes burned. Syd could not find out.

This is just a scare, I reasoned. I'll get her on birth control.

Juliet hid a person inside her with parts foreign to me. She was complex. She was a mystery under her skin.

I decided to walk. The movement helped my head, pounding from the night before. Movement would release the toxins. Long, fast strides to sweat the poison out.

To the bridge and back, I told myself.

I walked, phone growing sweaty in my hand. I walked under the sun. I walked toward the bridge. I walked quickly, then slowed my pace. I walked down the road, jumping every time I heard a car. I walked on the dusty shoulder. I looked up at the blue sky, down at the pebbles by my shoes. I walked, looking behind me at the rising and settling spumes of gravel dust.

Then I heard a truck coming. Ron honked and I jumped. Juliet in the passenger seat, looking straight ahead. He smiled and waved. And they kept going.

I went home and crawled back under the covers. I didn't want to move. I wanted darkness. Thoughts that weren't thoughts were welling up inside my chest and behind my eyes, black and red, black, then red.

223

thirty-five

224   The next morning, in the bathroom of our house, Juliet peed on a stick for the second time. She brought it out with her and said, "Can I see the first test?" She'd left it on her windowsill.

"Yeah, sure." I kept my voice light. Waited.

Minutes passed. She came back and said, "Pregnant."

"Let me look."

I took both tests, held them to the light. "Where are the instructions?"

I wasn't checking because I mistrusted the test. She handed me the box. It's that I didn't know what to say; my mind had frozen, just as it had before.

Outside the window the day had greyed, clouds sheeting the sky. Outside the window the mountains were obscured by clouds full of coming rain. "I'm going to make more coffee," I told Juliet, because the world didn't stop for every tragedy, even when I wished it could. "Will you have another cup if I make a pot?"

Not quite lunchtime. I got the coffee going and told Juliet I was going to run to the mailboxes. I slipped on my shoes, grabbed my phone from the counter, and left the house. A little way down the path, hidden by trees, I dialed Ron's number.

"Rose?"

"Juliet is pregnant."

A long silence. "Who's the father?"

"I don't know, we're still talking."

"Do you want me to come over?"

"Let me call you back."

Up the street I collected our bills, the offers for hearing aids, then returned to the house, through the back door into the kitchen. Clattered coffee cups.

"Here you go, hon." I set the coffee down in front of Juliet. The two of us sat across from each other at the table, a bowl of fruit and an open tub of margarine between us, looking at each other.

Now I had a gauge to study Juliet's choice, to live or die, by what she decided to do with the baby. To keep it was to turn toward life, to abort it was to point herself toward death. Maybe I could convince her to keep the baby. She'd give birth and we'd all live happily ever after. Juliet was a catalyst, to clean myself up. If I couldn't hold my own life together, how was I supposed to be a mother to someone else? She gave me a reason to try to stay sober. I'm more proud of Juliet than I've ever been of anything in my whole life. But then I remembered my own mother, and how my being on earth hadn't saved her, hadn't pointed her toward life. In that sense an abortion could be seen as a turn toward life—her own, the decision to abort, a recognition that she wasn't ready to have a baby and a way of looking out for her future—a future in which she was alive. I couldn't assume it meant she'd attempt suicide again—though you live your life always in the shadow of it happening again—anymore than I could assume it meant her turning toward life.

We sat drinking coffee. Juliet gave no indication of what she was thinking. To divine the future using Juliet's choice of whether or not to keep the baby as a gauge was the same as flipping a coin. A wrinkled tea towel hung from the stove handle next to yellow rubber gloves emptied of hands. A pine tree cast an angled shadow.

I leaned forward. "I want you to know I'm here to support you."

226

Maybe she hadn't heard or hadn't understood. Was she ignoring me? Or deliberating? "I don't want to push you, but at the same time, the faster we come to a decision, the better. Especially if you . . . you want to get an abortion." It was hard to see her in pain I would have given anything to carry. "I could call the clinic. A doctor's appointment. At least to get the results confirmed. That will be the first step."

She sighed.

"Do you want a hug?"

She nodded.

I gave her a hug.

"So. The dad," I said.

"I'll take care of it."

"Do you know?"

Juliet nodded.

"Ricky?"

She shook her head.

I paused, uncertain how to continue. "Someone I know?"

"Does it matter?"

"No. Yes."

Juliet played with the butter knife, stabbing the margarine, pulling it out of the tub, stabbing the margarine again. "Do you want to know?"

227

"If you want to tell me."

"Okay. Then, well. I guess I could tell you. This is so fucked up. I can tell you who the father is, but you can't tell Dad."

I nodded quickly. "That's a given."

"Dad's sick of me. I don't want to hurt him or you anymore. When you keep fucking up, no one in the family trusts you anymore."

This came as a surprise, a shock. I didn't know what to feel.

She looked at me so long I felt as if her eyes were X-raying my body, piercing my skin and cleaving the flesh from my bones.

"Jules. What are you telling me?"

"I can't do this anymore."

She told me the whole story, starting with his tuna boat and ending with his laundry-strewn bedroom. The same one I'd been in. I listened, a fire welling in my heart, bile rising, bitterness in my throat. The full horror took a moment to sink in. What had happened. How it had happened.

"Ron."

"Ron."

"Ron?"

She looked up, suddenly panic-stricken. "You won't tell Dad?"

"Honey, don't worry," I managed. "We'll figure this out." I shut my mouth and opened my arms: when someone you loved was in trouble that's what you did. I squeezed her tight, locking my wrist, pinning her arms to her sides so that she couldn't fight me but rather what supported her, just as when she was a toddler she'd rattle the bars of her crib or swing her weight back and forth in her high chair hating its confines, verging on a disastrous wipeout at every meal. I'd had a hard time resisting the temptation to set her free, sharing a need for growth, to do for herself and not be reliant on others.

And now my mind (a mind in chaos) performed mathematics to pinpoint love. Ron and I had slept together; he'd entered my soul. How can this be, a feeling proclaimed. Like a foreign object my body was now trying its best to expel, to express. But how could I express anything inside me? You're not allowed to gag on your own sins.

I listened to my daughter trying to figure out what kind of monster I was. She told me how surprised she'd been that day at the bridge when I let Ron take her home. How, when she'd taken a bath and then changed into the fresh set of clothes he'd given her, "I realized I was exactly where I needed to be."

Juliet had felt good on the boat, and good after, at Ron's house, flattered that he'd transformed a wheelbarrow into a barbecue and cooked her perfect chicken above arbutus wood. The next day she'd walked around in a towel after a shower, having washed three weeks of ocean salt from her hair. Cheeks scrubbed and tingling, she made herself at home in Ron's kitchen, reheating two cold cups of coffee in the microwave, moving through the space as though it were her own.

She brought the coffee into Ron's bedroom; he was in bed propped by cushions, reading the paper.

"Call your parents," he said. He smelled like scented candles. His gaze had the ring of truth about it.

"I will," she said. "Tomorrow."

At that moment in her story the sound of gravel under tires announced Ron's truck. His door squeaked open, in need of WD-40. The hair on the back of my neck stood up as he entered my house.

I took a mug shaped like an owl from the cupboard so I didn't have to face him. "Coffee?"

"Sounds good."

I added milk and a couple cubes of sugar, pushing it in front of him and when he sat down in the empty chair, I gazed at him. His muscles tightened. He knew I knew. He began to noticeably fidget, one moment slouched, the other unnaturally rigid, rubbing his sweaty palms on his knees. I crossed my arms, closing myself off from him, and took a sip of coffee. Juliet did the same but all the while looking at me, then exhaled and leaned back, putting her hand on his knee. "Dad's going to kill me."

I recoiled, short of breath, then quickly composed myself. "Juliet," I said, "can you give us a minute?"

Once she'd walked out onto the back porch, his leg began to shake. Then, after a moment of hesitation, he tried to explain. He actually used the word "consensual."

"I swear to God it was consensual."

"Explain to me how the fuck it can be consensual when she's suicidal."

The more he talked, rubbing one hand atop the other, the deeper the hole he dug. I asked him what kind of a sick person he was. He lowered his head as if in an attempt to hide something his eyes might give away. "I know how it looks."

His legs had not stopped moving. Oddly, a part of me felt sorry for him. "Tell me everything," I said, implying his confession would lessen my anger, and, maybe thinking he had dodged a bullet, he did. Palms up and pleading, he claimed, illogically, that Juliet had come on to him.

"So it's her fault?"

He became lost and confused as he tried to pick up his story again, repeating himself, his mind racing, panicking, he tried to figure out a way to explain without implicating himself further. His hand gestures grew larger and larger. He uncrossed his legs, rubbed his thighs with his hands, then crossed his legs again.

I shifted in my chair, looked away as he continued begging me to buy his story, overcome by a miasma of conflicting feelings that had surfaced. My own hopes had betrayed me, humiliated me. Love was as hollow as a con man who swindled with schemes that never worked out. I felt lost and jealous of my own daughter—who, as Ron failed to understand, was now in love with him.

"Do you love her?"

He nodded his head yes while saying, "No. Not like that."

I looked at him a long time and he returned my stare as if trying to ascertain whether I believed him or not. He was breathing heavily now like an animal in pain. From when he'd first invited her to visit his garden, building the trail, he'd been planning. I thought of the hours she'd spent among his strawberry plants.

"You used me," I said.

"No."

"You groomed me."

"No."

"How many times, Ron?"

"I swear. It's not like that."

"When did you start abusing her? When did you first touch my little girl?"

"It's not how it looks."

"What the fuck were you thinking?"

"This isn't about us," he said.

"You raped my little girl."

"What?"

"You groomed me. And you raped my little girl. You are not going to get away with this."

"Rose."

"I'm serious." I grabbed the butter knife from the tub of margarine on the table and pointed it at him.

"Rose," he said, "come on. It doesn't have to be like this. Can we just talk? Please?"

"Get the fuck out of my house," I said.

Ron turned, wringing his hands. "Fuck, have it your way." He called to Juliet out on the porch. "You coming?"

Juliet began crying. Sobbing. "Mom, it's not his fault." Huge sobs, her entire body shaking from the shoulders down. Then she followed him to the truck.

After they left, I went into the yard and sat on a plastic chair, preparing myself for what I would need to face. This time I couldn't tell myself that things were going to be okay. The moral complexity of birdsong, sunshine,

233

leaves coming off the walnut trees—everything was suddenly irreparable. Sometimes things couldn't be fixed, there were no spare parts in a drawer, and when you left this world all you left were your children. They were your legacy—and sometimes even they could not be put back together.

thirty-six

Syd got home from work. I leapt from the chair. The look on his face shifted into one of such deep concern that the shame of having slept with Ron, the very violence of my regret, sent me straight into his arms in a way that didn't feel untrue at all.

"What's the matter?" He held me.

"Ron." It was all I could get out.

"What? What happened?"

Not looking before I leapt, I shut my eyes tight. How many times had I done something only to regret it later?

"Rose. What is it?"

I should have told him the truth. I should have come clean.

"What did he do?" The words landed with the precision of a bird on a wire.

"I, it's just, at the hoedown and I was so drunk and when we went to get more beer in Ron's truck everything happened so fast and I couldn't breathe." I broke down in sobs. I knew I was loved. I knew I had everything a normal person could want—I had a good life in a rich world. The very ordinariness of my suffering vexed me; my body didn't feel like a temple.

I would punish Ron for what he'd done to Juliet. Even more, I would punish Ron and keep Juliet out of it.

And I would fall into Syd's arms like the trampoline they hold under a jumper, like the boat's net, fish leaping into it, like the fox into her den. Despite everything I'd run to him, drop everything, come empty-handed, empty as a flowerpot in the shape of want because I needed to hold on, breathing fire and smoke, columns of fire we built too hot to touch. We would thirst for each other, our passion consuming us, fingertips reaching across flames like God and Adam, reduced to ash over the skeleton of a busy city.

"Did he hurt you?"

I nodded. Syd would strike first and ask questions later; that's how he loved. "He gave me a beer, it must have had roofies. He raped me," I slurred, weeping. "Ron raped me."

A flash in Syd's head, a burst of colourful light as of a chemical explosion, blinding, burning instinct: to do the right thing. He looked at Juliet's door, and then he said nothing. He became ominously quiet. He paced, stared at an invisible spot on the kitchen table. Finally he said, "I want you to stay here."

"What are you going to do?"

"Stay here, Rose. I'm going to take care of this."

237

thirty-seven

238 Not even an hour later I sat on the couch, trembling, alone with my thoughts. What chance did Juliet have to learn empathy if anytime she brought me her problems I saw it as a character flaw and, at best, offered only solutions?

I never—once—listened.

The disgust I had for weakness, for a failure to deal with one's problems, made my body recoil. Juliet's propensity for making mountains out of molehills. Her enduring *neediness*.

Then my cell phone rang. It was Syd, saying what he wanted me to do just then.

I had no mercy. I didn't even understand the word. Was it the same thing as sympathy? Empathy? I didn't do as Syd asked. I'd been running too long. My body was worn down. I was a coward. Instead, I dropped the phone. I watched myself sit down at the kitchen table with my feet pointed toward the door, hands resting on my lap, a sombre look on my face. I couldn't face my own frailty. I didn't recognize the world at all.

Had Syd thought I wanted to follow Juliet around, watch her like a hawk on twenty-four-hour suicide watch? I'd changed, and not because I'd wanted to; a child who deserved much more than I had cast me in this role. I'd kept repeating, "I tried so hard," as if trying came with an award. The rationale that had propelled my internet searches had abandoned me. Even an animal distanced itself from the source of its suffering. After months of dissecting what had gone wrong, I'd come to believe that a person's response to mess only added to the entanglement. That the more you fought to get away the more the webs surrounded you, immobilized you.

There was only one way out of the trap. I could slice my jugular. Find a rope. Poison. A bottle of motor oil, drink the gas remaining in the three jerry cans under the deck, chug a gallon of house paint. I could eat the glass of broken fluorescent tubes. Smash one and swallow shards like potato chips. A hyper-awareness of seconds passing took over. I didn't have much time.

It occurred to me then that the mistake people made was in thinking they had all the time in the world.

thirty-eight

240   The bridge called to me. I glided down the path between silent alders, scented pines whose branches sprang from the shadows, scratching my face. I pushed them away. Easy steps, no going back.

An older couple on the bridge glanced at my face then quickly looked away. I paced from one end of the bridge to the other, back and forth, taking pictures of the shadows it cast on the water. I didn't blame myself for losing the fight: I'd fought hard, harder than I'd believed I could. Falling to the better opponent involved no disgrace. I'd picked myself up off the mat more than most, more than those who'd gone twelve rounds.

Grey and white seagulls carved through space, swirling above the waves against a background of clouds. I wanted a single stunning image of a seagull in flight: why was this difficult? Just one image. The challenge was tracking them as they bulleted across the sky. Grounded seagulls were fat, ugly birds. But in flight they were svelte, delicate, agile creatures able to glide up and down, hardly having to beat their wings. A link between the human and the angelic, the familiar and the divine. Shot after shot, I tried.

I took pictures not knowing why, certain only of the importance that someone in the future see what I was seeing right now: the water, extending its reach till it met the horizon, the birds, closer to heaven than children.

When Ron had twitched the ignition and peeled out of the driveway, a part of me had wanted to make a scene, wanted to run toward him, waving my arms, saying, "Stop, don't go," wanted help. My head was tangled into a thousand black knots it would take an entire sky to unravel.

I stopped pacing in the middle of the bridge, over the deepest part of the water. A woman on a bridge, without her family. I leaned over the railing as if trying to reel in the undertow. I leaned over the railing thinking sink or swim, thinking primal trauma. How many songs started with the saddest story in the world? You accepted this, you spent years with a Band-Aid in one hand and a Kleenex in the other, and the next thing you knew, your children were just . . . gone.

I leaned over the railing seeing everything. Families, joggers, cyclists, the older couple chatting together now as they watched a blue heron below. A sailboat, waves lapping a hull.

Kitesurfers. Kayakers.

When the sun shone, the scene turned the kind of white that made the horizon disappear.

Mist. Mountains.

An angler in a red ball cap and a windbreaker, the current jostling his rod.

Seagulls who thought of freedom as they soared.

A young boy at the water's edge, standing in the bridge's shadow. The water, a mirror of the day, seemed to go nowhere now. What did a bridge hope for?

The view wasn't what I'd hoped. Every forward step had brought me to where there were no more steps to take. Movement meant nothing here; this was the end of the line. The wind performed due diligence.

Flip a coin. Right. Wrong. Life or death. Hello or goodbye.

I wasn't only at the end of the line; I was tilted over it.

A woman on a bridge by herself, my aloneness all the keener for all those I saw who seemed to have family. Parents strolling along the shore, their children chasing each other in circles around them. Did they know how lucky they were?

242

I wrote Syd a text: "I've been living for others. Now I'm going to live for myself."

I reread the text and decided not to send it. I put my phone in my purse and in disgust, dropped the purse onto the bridge.

A falling fallen woman. No way out but down.

I hopped up so that I was sitting on the railing, my back toward the water. Sitting on the bridge took hardly any skill at all: deciding where one would end it, like deciding what restaurant to go to, had been the hard part. I just wanted to fly. Once. The wind pulled my hair across my face. I took pictures of two men in a boat wearing yellow vests.

The older couple hadn't batted an eye when I'd jumped up—if anything they continued to avoid my gaze, as if afraid of what they might see. To show weakness was a failure. Sympathy was weakness.

Fuck you, couple. Fuck you, tree. Fuck you, seagull. Fuck you, happy family. Fuck you, baby. Fuck you all.

The water was rocking and a light rain began to fall.

No coming back.

You threw away everything you needed to save, Rose. Yes.

I looked left, right, then raised myself to standing. A loud intense wind lifted the hair on my arms. Standing on the railing of the bridge, I was closer to heaven.

Now I was higher than the traffic. Now I could see across the bridge to the water beyond the hills. Now I could see past the iron and steel. Could see the low-hanging rainbow I'd missed that had been there all along.

My mother was my first lost battle. I tried to keep her alive and she died anyway. Fuck everyone who claims love conquers all.

I stood on my own two feet, continuing to hold till the last my position, then flung out my arms and leaned back into the wind. The wind could bear a load.

thirty-nine

Later I would learn that a Coast Guard vessel took Syd to the city harbour where a transport van waited to drive him to the police station downtown. During the ride every sharp stop jolted and battered him, flung him from one side of the van to the other. By the time he arrived at the station, bleeding from his lip, ranting about his rights, I had been wheeled into surgery. Detectives locked him into an interrogation room alone, chairs and a table, still wearing his bloody clothes, his hands still cuffed behind his back. A long time later detectives barged into the room as if they'd been the ones made to wait. The first thing he'd asked detectives was "How is Rose?" Next "How is Juliet?" Then "Are you charging me with murder?"

"Maybe. If he dies."

"He's alive. Oh, thank God. Thank God."

One of the detectives asked before leaving the inter-rogation room, "Do you need water? The bathroom? Is there anything I can do for you?"

Syd said, "He has family in India. Tell his wife I'm sorry. Tell his son I'm sorry."

Meanwhile the crime lab examined the blood-spatter on his sneakers and jeans.

Syd was brought to a holding cell, then up to the jail to be finger-printed and processed.

forty

Juliet had run blindly into the woods. When she came to the bridge she hid in the cedars, watching the currents, the eddies, the bits of wood churning like laundry in a washing machine. Juliet stood at the bottom of the bridge only to see me standing at the top of it, taking pictures. I didn't see her, not then.

But she saw me fall through the air, break the water's surface with a smack, and then disappear, gone. She stared at the spot I had been. I plunged into the depths then struggled to make my way to the surface, into an eddy's slow-moving water. And then a boat, and then a voice, and a man getting into the water. I felt something touch my leg. Juliet had jumped into the water too. Swam to me. We struggled, losing balance in the current as the icy water roared against my body. I saw Juliet at my side, telling me to fight; I tried to say, "It's too much." In the currents of a cold, cold river, in the waves, bobbing through the water, I saw images of Juliet's childhood: red Valentines, silver foil–wrapped hearts, yellow marshmallow chicks, orange pumpkins on a turquoise kitchen table, pink tutus, slippery blue mermaid tails. I heard my own voice through a tunnel explaining free will to Juliet in a hospital bathroom with handrails. I saw all the colours of the current pulling my life downriver; my life, glints on the river's surface like the reflection of a rainbow, beautiful, impossible to touch, all my memories just dots of colour now, stretching away from each other, growing and expanding, like the universe, away from me.

Juliet grabbed my hair. "Kick, Mom, kick!"

Struggling to stay afloat. I gasped for breath. We swam the last few feet completely underwater. I was laid out on the sand. Approaching sirens almost drowned out Juliet's words: "It's not normal but she's breathing."

forty-one

As soon as my feet left the railing, I regretted what I'd done. How many times had I leapt before I looked, only to regret what I'd done? I fell. Flying more than falling, like an umbrella in a gust, I fell. I turned in midair and hit the water with my feet. Underwater, I couldn't tell up from down. My constant desire to be elsewhere appeared ridiculous now—elsewhere was a lost place inside me, now tasting mud, now choking. I broke the surface. I tried to scream "Help me" but no sound came.

Then Juliet brushed my leg.

A paramedic with his blue latex gloves and his stethoscope, a woman lying on her back on the ground. Wet. Her sweater lifted. A breathing bag on her face. Me.

"What's her name? Rose? Can you hear me? Come on, Rose. Deep breath."

"Breathe, Mom. Breathe. Can you hear me? Don't stop breathing. I want you to never stop breathing. Just breathe."

forty-two

I jumped up from the couch. Juliet, in a rage, had flung open our door, denting the wall behind it with the knob. In the way I'd once felt her every roll or kick when she'd been part of my body, I felt her scream deep inside me: "MOM!"

Syd had pounded on Ron's door and pointed his rifle barrel at his head. He'd gestured with the rifle butt for Ron to sit down on the couch.

"You raping motherfucker," Syd said.

He glanced over at Juliet, who'd just emerged from the kitchen. Ron took that moment to step forward, his face a mask of confusion. "What the hell?"

"Don't talk or I swear to God I'll ram your nutsack down your throat." Syd turned back to Juliet.

"He never raped anyone," she pleaded.

"Stay out of this."

"What did Mom tell you? I swear it's not as bad as it sounds. Put the rifle down. You're scaring me. Dad. Please."

Syd pointed at the door with his rifle. "Go. Go home." Now the rifle scope wavered back to Ron.

"Only if you come with me, Dad. We'll go together, okay?"

"I have no choice here."

"Look, man." Ron raised his hands. "I'm no saint, but—"

"Daddy. I love him."

Syd, disoriented now. "What are you *talking* about?"

Only then did he spit out my accusation of rape. And only after that did Ron admit to our affair.

Juliet erupted. "My *mom*? What do you *mean*, my mom?"

And then, after that, the whole truth came out. Juliet and Ron. Ron and me.

And now Juliet stood, shaking, before me. "WHAT THE FUCK HAVE YOU DONE?"

What the fuck, Rose?

I talked softly though it was difficult with her inches from my face, staring right at me.

The pitch of her voice rose. "I hate you, I hate you, I hate you." Juliet pulled her hair and made a shrieking sound.

There was no coming back from this. You threw away everything you needed to save, Rose.

Yes.

Juliet stormed out the door. I sat back down on the couch, trembling, alone with my thoughts, the reality of what I'd done, and the horror of what would come next, not only sinking in but crashing down on my shoulders. My phone rang. Syd. "I shot Ron. Tell Andrea I shot Ron. Tell her to come get me. I'll be waiting. Tell her I won't be any trouble."

I had the rest from a few different sources, including the police detectives who, as I lay in my hospital bed, wanted to know what role I'd played in Syd's going to Ron's. In what way had I instigated the misery Syd had been carrying? Was I an accessory to his crime?

Syd couldn't look at Ron's body lying on the living room floor. He got a blanket from the bedroom and covered the body with it but then he couldn't look at the blanket either, and so he stepped outside and sat on the porch.

Andrea might shoot him if she saw the rifle.

Syd walked to the head of the driveway and lay his weapon down. Then he walked back to the porch and waited. Feeling as though someone was behind him. He lit a cigarette. Then another. By the time his phone rang he'd smoked seven cigarettes, paced to the end of Ron's driveway and back, closed his eyes, opened them, and thought about getting into his truck and driving right into the river.

He'd expected the police, but the voice said, "Am I speaking to Sydney Barrow?" When he heard what came next the porch tilted beneath him, his boots sounding on the slats before his legs buckled, dropping him to his knees.

"She's jumped."

The paramedic in blue latex gloves put a plastic tube up my nose. Another clipped a cord to my finger and slid what looked like a snowboard beneath my back. Juliet pushed him away. "This is my *mom*," she said, and held my hand as she jogged with the stretcher, between the paramedics, to the trailhead where a gurney waited to rush me past the crowds in the parking lot. And now somehow Andrea was there among them. I closed my eyes and became aware only of a bustle in the background, the sound of an air ambulance approaching. It would take me to the clinic, a voice said.

Andrea's walkie-talkie crackled. Ron had come to and called 911—the bullet had missed his heart and gone into his left shoulder. Then Andrea was gone again, a second ambulance dispatched.

Syd pushed his way through the clinic door, swore at one of the paramedics who said he'd call security, and fought his way to the gurney. *She's jumped.* He was expecting to see Juliet. When he saw it was me, he stared in stupefaction.

I said, "I'm sorry."

I remember the *br-r-r-r-r-r* of the helicopter, the rolling sound like a Spanish love song I'd once danced to in a bar late one summer night, and the doctor saying, "Who's going? There's only room for one."

Syd and Juliet, running alongside the stretcher toward the helicopter, Syd on one side, Juliet on the other, and with me in the middle, as always. They looked at each other over my body.

"You go," Juliet said.

Syd was about to get in. Then Andrea returned with more paramedics and Ron on a stretcher.

"Syd, step away. Show me your hands."

I remember the helicopter ride. Then darkness. Then, sometime later, a stuffed cat on the sill of a square window, and Juliet. I remember Juliet.

forty-three

Juliet sets a geranium plant on the nightstand. She's cut off her eyelashes to appear less feminine. She has the look of an avenging angel ready to smite for honour. She's done a sketch of my nurse with a witch's nose, a crone, pointing an angry finger at me, cartoon-style, under the caption "No Smoking."

"Open your hand. Close your eyes," she says.

Juliet puts something small and soft in my palm, closes my fingers over it, then lets go. I open my hand. Cloth. The last scrap of her Chinese bathing suit, shaped like the state of Texas.

"It's not for keeps. I'm only lending it to you. Remember that book?"

"I do. The story began with a boy and his blanket."

"And it ended," Juliet says, "with the blanket becoming a button for a mouse."

The story was about how the boy, who carried his security blanket the way other children carried a rabbit's foot, was ultimately able to pass on a token of himself, however frayed and shrunken with age.

"I will hold it to my cheek," I chant, "among the beeping machines."

Between Juliet's visits I watch TV—hospital shows, true crime shows, shows all about rescues. Good triumphing over evil. Redemption. Following the right instructions to bring back the dead. CPR prevailing. Courage and Hope through science. A solution for everything. Good people doing stupid things, and stupid people becoming heroes. Mistakes turning out okay. Shows that distill life into a twenty-minute script—the only twenty minutes that matter when a mountain climber has fallen off a cliff or a drinker needs a new liver. I see now that these shows allow me to draw death near while keeping it at arm's length. A paramedic, asked about a motorbike accident victim, defends the rider's freedom: "If you're not living on the edge you're taking up too much room."

I don't know if my fear that Juliet will take her own life will ever go away. But I know what I've lived through. Although what I brought back from those dark lands adds nothing to the wisdom of the world. Our lives touch others. We have understood our connection to each other for millennia. We're joined at the hands, at the feet, at the hip. We are one unbroken chain going back to the beginning of time. Humanity, a string of paper dolls.

"I saw Ron. I went down there."

My heart lurches. "Did you talk to him?"

"Hell, no. I just kind of stood at the door. Thought maybe I'd wait until he was sleeping and unplug him."

"Me first."

"Too bad it would only be his iPad."

Juliet flips to the music station. She doesn't like reality shows. "Too much tension," she says.

The TV plays an all-girl band wearing ripped stockings and black leather bracelets. "Last chance to dance," Juliet says, using the remote as a microphone. "Come on, Mom. Live a little. Do the wave!"

"No thanks."

"*Let it roll, let it ride,*" she sings along. "Come on, Mom, you're not dead yet. *Come on over to the other side.* Yeah, Mom! That's it. Woop-woop. Do the wave!"

I used to wonder how my mother, a shy, overweight girl who met my father in college, had become a haunted figure looking out the window, hands on a book on her lap, pages unturned. How she'd become so broken.

The story of how they met had come to me in bits and pieces: my father, ex-military, and my mother, with a small group of friends at a bar. They didn't talk to each other, at least not that first night. My mother could only gaze, enamoured, too nervous to do more. When she saw my father again, she resolved to speak to him; the two of them ended up going back to her apartment. They began kissing. Then things took a turn. My mother said, "Don't." My father said, "Shut up," and forced himself onto her. Afterward, my mother, bleeding and in pain, called a friend who came over and advised her to phone the police. But no. Instead my mother called a nurse who lived in her building, who examined her and said she'd be okay after a few days of bedrest. The nurse, too, begged her to call the police. My mother was stubborn, though. She felt it was her fault: and what would people think of a girl who invited a man in and kissed him and then said no? Sometime later my father would phone and offer her money to offset the trouble, saying he'd never drink again, apologizing profusely. They began dating. Both seemed to think they were helping the other get through a bad time.

I understand better now, I think, that faraway stare out the window, searching the horizon for something lost. I'd often asked myself what I could have done. Could I have been a better child? Would that have made my mother more robust? Durable enough to withstand the hurt of looking into a mirror and finding only emptiness? What does it mean to keep a child of rape?

I took responsibility, not just for my mother's death—mathematically, only a single day in a lifeful of days—but each and every day leading up to that catastrophe. I carried the blame for her sadness.

I could be happy and drunk, or sad and sober. Clean but sad. High but happy. What would you choose? "Is that what you meant by too happy?" I ask. "Hey, Jules? I get it now. About the cherries. You know? When you said everyone expects you to have cherries?"

Everyone expects you to be healthy, more than healthy, *strong*.

Will Juliet's child look into the mirror and wonder, What part is rapist and what part is me?

How will I comfort Juliet, if I talk of love at all—about how it pulls you under like whitewater, spits you up downriver, wounded, tired and confused, full of awkward silences? What can I say about the gap between what we want and what we get? What can I say that hasn't been said a thousand times before?

That's the thing about emptiness. That's the thing about desire. You have to let go, but not of the edge. To be free we let go of desire itself. The right to judge. This against that, good against bad. We become clean as a bowl, empty as bamboo, hollow as a golden wedding band. Only then can you lose everything you love and keep going.

On the day I tried to kill myself I walked quickly to the bridge, tongue-tied, half-dazed, losing my shoe in the forest. I felt no words, just a tragic desire to be rescued. I remember a bird's-eye view of a fence, laundry on it, cutting between two hills spotted with scrub brush, like an unshaven chin. I remember the height. I remember falling. Light spilled into my eyes and I remember thinking, Is this heaven?

261

Juliet stops dancing. "Talked to Dad yet?"

"No. But thanks for giving him the number."

"Yeah." Juliet looks puzzled. "No worries. So Dad didn't call?"

"Nope." My heart sinks. I don't want to think about Syd calling, or not, and what it means that he's in police custody.

She reaches for my hand and squeezes it the same way I'd squeezed her hand the morning we sat in the emergency room triage, wishing there was more I could do. But sometimes the hold of a hand is enough—enough to let you know that you're doing okay, that the other person is okay.

―――――――

Syd will do his time in max security, in a pen too far away for me to visit often. On the day he's released I'll be the last person he calls. And after our call, a week will pass before the next one. After that, Syd will call every day.

I'll call Juliet. Juliet, married by now, with children. She will meet her father for coffee at a cheap family restaurant.

Because that's how we do things. We move on. We'll pick up the pieces and wait for time to scatter our broken hearts over a field to watch something grow. The present plants me like a flag in that distant country, and as long as Juliet's there, I'll be there, too. Watching her shine with the glory of movement and possibility.

I'll be there, standing tall.

I'll be there. Waving.

acknowledgments

Thank you to Steve Barrie and my parents for their grocery deliveries and unending support, my agent Denise Bukowski, so like the Zen masters of old, my soul-sister and editor and Nicole Winstanley for keeping the faith through nail-biting moments, Meredith Pal and Karen Alliston for their work in refining the prose; Yvette Guigueno, my sister from another mother, who, of all my friends, is the one I most want to make proud; Antonio Michael Downing aka John Orpheus for reading early drafts, 12 Midnite for making "Never give up," my slogan, Thembelihle Moyo whose voice became my light, Sid Chow Tan for always having a smoke for me, may your journey be peaceful. Special thanks goes out to Jet Starkey for the laptop, Adrienne Wetmore who helped me find a different ending, Syd and Rose from Mayne Island, BC, who had nothing to do with the Syd and Rose of this book but had the best couple name ever. Bigups to the Canada Council for the Arts and the BC Arts Council for providing much of the funding for this project.

YASUKO THANH's story collection *Floating Like the Dead* was shortlisted for the Danuta Gleed Award and the Ethel Wilson Fiction Prize and named a *Quill & Quire* Best Book of the Year. *Mysterious Fragrance of the Yellow Mountains*, her debut novel, won the Atwood Gibson Writers' Trust Prize for Fiction, the City of Victoria Butler Book Prize, and was nominated for the Amazon First Novel Award. Thanh's memoir, *Mistakes to Run With*, was a national bestseller. She lives in Victoria, B.C.